DARE

A Bradford Academy Novel

Rowdy Rooksy

RowdyGunnshy Productions

SPECIAL THANKS

Shout out to my business partner, writing partner and necessary but unwanted accountability coach, C. L. Gunn. You're a pusher. It's annoying. It's necessary. So, I thank you!

To my partner and love. You know who you are. Thanks for always supporting me and telling me I can do anything. You were right.

AUTHOR'S NOTE

Dare is a reverse harem, high school bully romance. This means that our female main character, Fallon Gamble, has multiple love interests. It also means that for a large portion of this book, the love interests and other characters aren't the nicest to Fallon. Please know that this book does not condone or romanticize bullying in any way.

Any make-out sessions or sexual situations featuring Fallon are consensual. And while this book is about high school students, this is not your typical young adult novel. The characters are ruthless, profanity is a staple and these are young adults so emotions are on overload. The story contains underage drinking, some drug use, sexual situations and other adult scenarios. None of the characters in this book are under the age of seventeen.

WELCOME TO BRADFORD ACADEMY

Tucked in the tall, rugged hills of limestone and granite in Texas Hill County sits Bradford Academy, boarding school for the off-spring of Texas's elite. Bradford Academy houses and shapes the minds of the sons and daughters of Senators, oil tycoons, large ranch owners and foreign billionaires. These kids are filthy rich, entitled and authority means nothing to them. They can have anything they want, go anywhere they want and do anything they want. Even get away with murder.

CHAPTER ONE

There's nothing like the stench of death. It's rank and pungent with a sickening sweetness. It's the smell that surrounds my mother as she lays dying in her hospital bed. It's a smell I'll never forget.

Mom found out she had cancer a year ago. The disease came out of nowhere and took over her life fast. We were both really shocked when she was diagnosed seeing how she lived such a healthy lifestyle. She was a vegetarian and worked out daily. Mom treated her body like a temple so I just couldn't wrap my head around how something like fucking cancer was even allowed to enter her body let alone live there and destroy it.

She's been in the hospital for the past two weeks and there's no sign of her coming out of this alive. Every day she looks more emaciated. The once perfectly smooth and glowy brown skin of her face is now ashen and dull. Her amber eyes that used to light with happiness are now shadowed in pain and sadness.

I sit in the chair next to her hospital bed. It's been my spot every day after school since she was admitted. I'm so worried about her. What am I going to do if she dies? She's the only family I have. My father died before I was born so I never knew him and mom said he came from a very small family. Just him and his parents who are both dead. So, yeah, it's been me and my mom all these years and now she's dying.

Mom gave me the best life she could. We had a modest three

bedroom house on the West side of Omaha, Nebraska. Mom owned a yoga studio with a full roster of classes and clients so she was able to pay the bills, keep food on the table and give me everything I needed. And we were close. She was my best friend. We shared everything. She taught me everything; how to ride a bike, how to cook, how to drive, yoga. She helped me get ready for my first dance, gushed with me after my first kiss and comforted me after my first breakup. She's been there for all of my firsts and I have so many more of them to come and she won't be there. The realization hits me like a brick and I can't help the tears that well in my eyes. I don't want to wake mom so I hold in my sobs as tears run a silent trail down my cheeks.

"Fallon," my mother calls, her voice thin and weak.

I wipe the tears from my cheeks with the back of my hand and will myself to get it together. She's already in so much pain. The last thing I want to do is add to it by having her see me cry. "Yes, mamma?" I say, trying to add some brightness to my voice but the words just come out choked.

"Come here," she says, her fingers tapping the empty space on the bed next to her.

I move stiffly to the bed and sit down, folding my hands in my lap. That overwhelming stench of death is more potent now. Maybe because I'm so close to her. I don't know but the smell surrounds me, invading my nostrils, choking me.

"I don't want you to be sad, Fallon. Things happen in life that we can't control. Death is one of them. And we both know I'm dying."

"Mamma," I say trying to cut her off. I don't want to hear her talk about dying because saying it makes it that more real. I know she's dying but I haven't uttered the words out loud. I just didn't want to put them in the air. I didn't want to give life to them. To make them real.

"Fallon, please. I don't have much time left and I need you to come to terms with the fact that I won't be here much longer."

"Mamma, you don't know that. You could get better. Miracles happen."

She smiles but it doesn't quite reach her eyes. "I know you want that to be true but, baby girl, but you and I both know what's happening here and before I go there's something I need to tell you." She grabs my hand; her hold is weak.

I wrap my hands firmly around hers needing the connection.

"All your life it's been you and me. My parents died young so you never knew them and I didn't have any siblings or other family. And your father died before you were born so you never got the chance to know him either."

"Or his family," I add.

Mamma closes her eyes and lets out a heavy sigh before opening them again. "That's what I want to talk to you about," she says.

I look at her curiously. What could she possibly have to talk to me about a family who's all dead?

"Fallon, your father did die in a terrible accident but there's something you should know."

"What," the words a whisper on my lips. An unease settles in my stomach as I wait for her to speak.

"Your father didn't come from a small family and his parents aren't dead."

Suddenly I'm blanketed in a wave of shock and confusion. *Did I hear her right? Did she say that my father's parents aren't dead? My Grandparents are alive?* Tears sting the back of my eyes. How could she lie to me all these years? She knew what not having a father did to me growing up. Being bi-racial and having a hard time knowing how and where to fit in. Looking too black for some and not enough for others. She knew how empty I felt not having a family - cousins, uncles, grandparents. Watching all my friends with their mothers and fathers at parties and school functions or them going away to spend the summer with their grandparents. I longed for all those things growing up. And to find out now that I could have had them is just devastating.

"Fallon, I'm sorry I lied to you all these years but you don't understand everything that happened."

"So, tell me," I say, trying not to sound too harsh, too angry.

Pain and sorrow worry her face and she looks away for a minute. "Your father was an amazing man. I always told you that. What I didn't tell you was that he came from a very wealthy family in Texas. I told you how we met. He was in town on business and we met at the coffee shop I was working at. Remember?"

I nod. Of course, I remember. She used to tell me stories about my dad all the time when I was young. About how handsome and smart he was. How in love they were. How much I look like him. How I have his green eyes. "You were young, just nineteen. And you were working at the coffee shop part-time while studying to be a yoga instructor," I say.

She smiles, this time it reaches her eyes. "Yeah, and your father, he was so handsome and charming. He swept me right off my feet. We dated long-distance for a while. He came back and forth to Omaha often. We were so in love." She stares off for a minute as the memories overtake her. "His last visit was amazing. We stayed in my studio apartment all weekend, talking, laughing, and making love. He told me he wanted to marry me and that he had a few things he needed to straighten out back home first. So, he left and he said he'd be back the following weekend but he never showed up. I called him so many times but all my calls went unanswered. I didn't understand it, why he'd ignore my calls, why he'd desert me. I knew he loved me. I knew it. So, I did some research and found out who his family was and I called his parent's house. His mother answered. She asked who I was and I told her that I was Tennison's girlfriend, that I lived in Nebraska and that we were in love. She became enraged, calling me terrible names and saying that everything was my fault. That he was dead and it was my fault. Tennison's father took the phone from her and told me never to contact them again. A month later I found out I was pregnant with you and I had a choice to make. I didn't know your father's family and they were so horrible to me when I called that I decided it was best that I raise you on my own. I would give you his last name and tell you about your father the way that *I* knew him." She stares off for a minute a soft smile on her thin, dry lips.

I supposed she's thinking of him.

The smile slowly fades and her eyes hold a certain sadness.

One that's laced in regret. "His parents were so awful to me. They blamed me for Tennison's accident and I didn't want them to resent you too so I made up the story that his parents were dead. That way you wouldn't ever ask about them or want to see them, get to know them. I know it sounds bad but I did what I thought was best. Hell, maybe me getting sick is karma for keeping you away from your father's family."

"Don't say that momma. It wasn't right what you did but you did the best you could." I say, squeezing her hand. Yes, I was angry and confused but she was my mom, the only parent I had and no matter what I love her.

"I just don't want you to hate me, baby girl."

"I could never hate you. You gave me such a good life. I'm lucky to have had you." I say as the tears I was holding back crash over the edge and come tumbling down my face.

"Come here," she says, motioning for me to lay next to her.

I climb in the bed and snuggle next to her laying my head on her shoulder. She wraps her arm around me and simply hugs me as I cry. And I'm crying for so many things. I'm crying for my mother who's dying, for my father who's dead and for me living all this time and not knowing that my father's family was alive and out there somewhere. I cry for a good while and momma says nothing. She just holds me until my tears subside.

"I'm glad you know the truth, Fallon. Because," she pauses for a few seconds, "I'm dying and you're still young, just barely seventeen. You're still in high school. You need a family. You need someone to take care of you."

I look at her, searching her weary face. "What are you saying, momma?"

"I reached out to your grandfather. I sent him a letter telling him about you. Of course, he wanted a paternity test. Remember your physical last year, they did a cheek swab on you."

I nod. It's all I can do. I'm too shocked to speak.

"They don't do cheek swabs for physicals, Fallon. That swab was used for a paternity test. The results came back a near perfect match which I knew they would. Your grandmother has already passed on but your grandfather is alive and wants to have a relationship with you. He's agreed to take you in once I'm gone."

"But momma-" she cuts me off.

"No buts, Fallon. You need someone to take care of you after I'm gone. And your grandfather, Wilson Gamble, can do that. He's one of the wealthiest men in Texas and can give you a life I never could."

Wilson Gamble? My grandfather's name is Wilson Gamble and he's some uber wealthy guy in Texas that my mom wants to ship me off to after she's dead. This is just crazy. Instead of planning my future with some grandfather I don't know, she should be worrying about her present. She should be fighting to get better so she can be there to see me grow up. To see me get married and have children. I'm going to need her when those things happens.

I lift up and stare down at her in disbelief. "What are you taking about? You gave me a great life, momma. I don't need some rich, old geezer who blamed you for my father's death to come save me. I don't care how rich he is."

"Fallon, you're still a child. Who's going to take care of you when I'm gone?"

"First of all, stop saying that. You can still get better. You just have to want to," I reason.

"Fallon, I have stage four cancer. I can't walk. I can't feed myself. Baby girl, I'm dying," she says, placing her hand over mine.

"I won't be here much longer and I have to know that you'll be cared for once I'm gone."

"I don't need some stranger taking care of me. I'll take care of myself. I'm smart and resourceful," I argue.

"How will you eat? How will you pay the bills?"

"I'll get a job."

"And finish high school? No, I won't have it. You've already had to deal with so much lack in your life. You have the chance to live a better life. To not have to struggle. You can go to college and be and do whatever you want."

"What does all that matter if you're not here?" I say.

"It matters because I'll die knowing you'll be taken care of. That you won't have to struggle the way I did. I know I made it look easy, kid, but it was hard being a single parent. I just want better for you. You're such an amazing young woman. You're going to do so many great things. I know it. Now promise me you'll go with your grandfather when I'm gone. Promise me you'll go and you won't put up a fight."

I stare at my mother laying there in that hospital bed looking like a shell of the woman I knew. I want to be mad at her. I want to lash out but I can't. She's already in so much pain and I can't bear to add to it. So, I lay my head on her shoulder and say, "Okay, mamma. I promise."

Things escalated quickly after that day at the hospital. Mamma's condition got worse and she slipped into a coma. Three days later she was dead.

Momma's business partner, Shannon Nichols, took care of the funeral arrangements. It's a simple yet beautiful service held at the small church me and momma sometimes attended. All of momma's clients from her yoga studio are in attendance plus all of her close friends.

I sit in the front pew quiet, still, numb. Shannon sits next to me holding my hand. She's such a kind woman, very caring. She looked after me when momma went into the hospital, paying the bills and making sure I had food in the house. I'm very thankful for her.

The service is fairly short. Pastor Johnson gives a great sermon and a beautiful eulogy. I'm so numb and dazed, I'm surprised I even heard it.

The ride to the cemetery is surreal. It's like I'm watching it all happen. Like my consciousness left my body and is floating up above me watching as I sit in the back of the car with Shannon.

My body is on autopilot as I exit the car and take my seat in the row of chairs that are lined up in front of a massive hole in the ground. I stare blankly as pallbearers carry my mother's casket and place it on the metal frame with straps. I watch numbly as Pastor Johnson says a few words before the casket is lowered into the ground. It's over. She's gone and all I can do is sit there, numb and not moving.

"Fallon, honey," Shannon's soft voice floats over to me. "It's time. We have to go."

I look at her. I can't find my voice so I plead with her with my eyes. We can't leave yet. We can't leave her. I can't leave her.
She seems to understand. She places her arm around my shoulder and hugs me to her side. I lay my head on her shoulder and she strokes my hair. We sit like that until the driver comes over and tells us he has to get back to the funeral home. It's time to go.

Reluctantly, I allow Shannon to lead me to the car. It's not until we drive away that tears start to fall from my eyes.

CHAPTER TWO

We go straight from the cemetery to Shannon's house where the repass is being held. Everyone from the funeral is there and there is enough food to feed a small village.

People keep coming up to me giving me their condolences and all I can do is stare blankly at them. Shannon tries to get me to eat but I just stare at the plate she sits in front of me not taking a single bite. I can hear everyone around me whispering. What will she do now? Where will she go? Who will take care of her? All of the chatter is starting to get to me. I have to get out of here. I jump up from the couch, the plate that is sitting on my lap goes flying. All talking stops as everyone turns to look at me. Eyes of sadness, eyes of concern, eyes of pity all looking at me. All waiting for me to break. And I'm on the verge too, of breaking. But I won't do it here. Not in front of all of their sad, concerned, pitying eyes.

I look at Shannon. We lock eyes and she gives me a slight nod as if she knows that I need to get out of here. And I do. I get out of there as fast as I can. In fact, I run. I run out the door and down the street and I don't stop running until I make it home. I can barely get my house key into the lock because my hands are shaking so badly. When I do finally get through the door I run straight to momma's room and throw myself on her bed and wail. I'm talking loud, deep, guttural cries. I can't tell you how long it went on I just know that I wake up the next morning to Shannon gently shaking me awake.

"Fallon, honey," she says as she gently shakes my shoulder.

I blink my eyes open, frowning at the sunlight coming through the windows.

"I opened the curtains. It's such a beautiful day out. I thought it would do you some good to see the sunlight," Shannon says, a gentle smile tipping her lips up at the corners.

I rub my eyes. They're tender to the touch. I was crying all night so I'm sure they look just as bad as they hurt.

"How do you feel?" Shannon asks.

I try to speak but my mouth is dry. I clear my throat and the words come out on a hoarse whisper. "I don't know. Sad. Numb."

"The pain will soften as time goes by. It'll be hard at first. You'll miss her terribly but try to focus on the good times you had with her and eventually you'll smile when you think of her."

I don't say anything. Right now, I can't think of any moment in time when I won't think of my mother and cry. In fact, I'm doing my best to hold back tears right now.

Shannon gets off the bed and moves a few feet away. "Fallon, I came to check on you, to make sure you were alright but I also came because…," she pauses and looks out the window.

"Because what?" I ask.

"Because your grandfather is here. He arrived early this morning. You mother gave him my information some time ago. He reached out the day of the funeral saying he would be in town the next day, today, to get you and take you to Texas."

"What?" I croak out as I shoot up in bed. "He's here? Already?" I scramble out of the bed. "What about the house? Mamma's things? My things? What about my friends? School starts in a few weeks? I can't go with him."

I'm pacing the floor and Shannon follows my every move, her hands clasped in front of her belly. "Fallon, please, you have to calm down."

"Calm down! Calm down! I just buried my mother yesterday and this stranger wants to whisk me away from everything that reminds me of her. I'm not leaving. I'm not going with him."

"Fallon, please, it's what your mother wanted. And don't worry about your stuff. I'll pack up the house and send you whatever items you want. Everything else, I'll put in storage.

Okay?"

No, not okay. Nothing is okay. My mom is dead. My entire life has been turned upside down and now I have to move to another fucking state and live with a grandfather I've never met. A grandfather who hated my mother because he held her responsible for his son's death.

Sickness fills my belly. I hold my breath to keep from vomiting. My fingers curl into fists at my sides and tears sting my eyes. I wobble in my stance and grind my heels into the carpet in an attempt to keep standing but my knees buckle. They just give way and I sink down to the floor and the terrible sobbing starts again.

Shannon rushes over, folds me in her arms and gently rocks me. "I'm sorry, Fallon. I'm so sorry," she whispers over and over again.

After a while my sobs subside and all I feel is hallow. I know I can't stay here. As much as I want to, I know I can't. I'm seventeen with no job and no money of my own. And as much as I'd like to believe that I can take care of myself, I can't. Mom always took care of me and no matter how sad or angry I am, I made a promise to her. I promised that after she died I would go live with my grandfather and that I wouldn't put up a fight about it.

Slowly, I disentangle myself from Shannon who stares tentatively at me.

"I'm going to go shower. I at least want to look halfway presentable when I meet my grandfather for the first time," I say then turn and leave my mother's room.

I take a long shower, trying to scrub the past few days away. It doesn't work. When I get out the shower and wipe the steam off the mirror, the same sullen face that has become a little too thin and little too pale looks back at me. It was only a few months ago that my skin was a vibrant cafe' au latte, my cheeks were flushed with a natural pinkish color and my eyes were a bright, happy green. Mom use to say they sparkle. Now they're just dull green orbs.

I dress plainly in a pair of jeans and a white t-shirt. I don't bother to dry my hair so it hangs in soppy wet rings around my head and shoulders. I make my way downstairs. I can hear Shannon and a male voice talking softly.

"How is she?" the male voice asks. His voice is deep with a slight southern accent.

"About as expected. She was very close with her mother," Shannon replies.

"I can imagine, seeing that's the only parent she had but the sooner I get her out of here the better. She'll heal faster in a different environment. She'll have every resource at her disposal. I've already scheduled sessions with a trusted therapist. She'll be fine in no time." the man finishes as if that settles everything.

Anger swells in me at his words. A different environment won't change anything. What the hell is he talking about? I have the urge to run back upstairs, lift up my bedroom window and sneak out like I used to do when mom thought I was sleeping. And I almost do. I turn and take a few steps back up the stairs when my mother's words float through my mind.

Promise me you'll go with your grandfather. Promise me you won't put up a fight.

I squeeze my eyes shut and take a deep breath. I have to do this. I have to keep my promise. I have to go with my grandfather.

I turn around and slowly make my way down the stairs. Shannon and my grandfather, are standing in the middle of the living room. My grandfather's back is to me. He's tall with a decent build. Not too thin, not too thick. His greying hair is tapered in the back and he's wearing an expensive, tailored suit.

Shannon looks up at me on the stairs triggering him to turn around and look at me too.

My breath hitches in my throat as my eyes clash with eyes the same emerald color as mine. I study his face. Besides the green eyes, I don't think I look much like him. I will say he's handsome for an old man. He's got a perfectly straight nose, a nice angular jaw and very good eye brows. And he's distinguished looking too.

"Hello," I whisper as I make my way down the rest of the stairs.

"Hello, Fallon," he says. He walks over and meets me just as I make it down the last step. He stretches his hand towards me. "I'm Wilson Gamble, your grandfather."

I stare at his outstretched hand. I thought it would be wrinkled or marred with age spots but it's not. His hand is a nice fleshy peach color and it's smooth. Reluctantly, I take it.

"I know this must all come as a shock to you. Losing your mother and finding out that you have a living grandparent but I want you to know I'm going to look after you. You're my son's daughter. You're family. My family. And the Gambles take care of their own."

My grandfather doesn't waste any time getting me out of Nebraska. I literally pack a few of my clothes, some pictures of me and mom, some of her jewelry and before I know it we're on his private jet headed to Texas.

A black Rolls Royce Phantom is waiting for us on the tarmac as soon as the plane touches down. My grandfather and I didn't talk at all on the plane. He started working as soon as we boarded and I curled up in my plush leather seat and went to sleep. I slept the entire plane ride. I guess I was still exhausted from my so-called life over the past few weeks.

We don't speak on the drive to my grandfather's house. He talks quietly into his cell phone conducting business while I stare out the window at the passing scenery. Based on the signs whizzing by, we're in Houston. We stay on the highway, zipping through traffic and passing several tall buildings which I assume means we're passing through downtown. We drive for a while and the major traffic starts to fall away as we enter a residential area. We pass large houses or I guess you would call them estates because all I see is sprawling mansions surrounded by perfectly manicured lawns, protected by massive iron gates.

The car slows and comes to a stop in front of a pair of large golden gates with a large G situated in the middle. The gate opens slowly and the car crawls through. As we cruise up the driveway my eyes saucer as a massive mansion comes into view. It looks like one of those French palaces I saw in a documentary we watched in French class last year. It's all grand and splendor and the landscaping is gorgeous. The lawn is lush, green and beautiful and vibrant trees are scattered perfectly throughout the property. I swear it's something out of a magazine.

"We're here," my grandfather says as the car comes to a halt.

The driver opens the back door and my grandfather gets out. I follow behind him and stand awkwardly next to the car.

"Don't worry about your bags. Aaron will bring them in."

I look at the driver whose name, I guess, is Aaron. He gives me a half smile and a nod then moves to the trunk to get my bags.

"This way, Fallon," my grandfather says, motioning for me to follow him.

The doors to the mansion open without my grandfather having ever touched the door handle.

"Welcome home, Mr. G," a black woman, much older than my grandfather, greets him then looks at me. Warmth emanates from her. She smiles and says, "Hello, Fallen. Welcome home."

I just look at her unsure of what to say.

"This is Phyllis. She's been with the family since I was a child. She'll show you to your room and get you whatever you need."

"Thank you," I whisper. I still haven't quite found my full voice.

"Well, I have some work to do. I'll see you at dinner. We can talk then," he says then hurries away.

I'm left standing there wondering what I should do.

Phyllis walks over. "This must all be very overwhelming for you, child. C'mon, let me show you to your room. I think you're going to like it."

I let her usher me through the massive house. She points out different rooms as we pass by them. The place has a bowling alley, a racquetball court, a mini movie theater, a private gym with a sauna and a huge veranda that can easily seat a hundred people for dinner. It's spectacular. Under normal circumstances I would be going out of my mind with excitement but these aren't normal circumstances. I just lost my mom. I'm not sure if things will ever be normal again.

Phyllis stops in front of a set of tall double doors. "This is your room," she says pushing the doors open.

I cannot believe my eyes. The bedroom is huge. It's literally half the size of my entire house back in Nebraska. Everything in the room is purple and white which is cool becasue purple is my favorite color. Two points for granddad on that one.

There's a huge four poster bed with an expensive looking comforter and a mountain of pillows that's the centerpiece of the room. Everything else sort of flows around it. On one side of the room there's a bookshelf built into the wall. It's filled with books and next to it is a long window seat with a cushion that matches the comforter on the bed. There's a set of double doors on the other side of the room that lead out to a terrace.

"It's a lovely room. Perfect for a teenage girl," Phyllis says from behind me.

"It's really nice," I say looking over my shoulder at her. I move towards the double-doors leading to the terrace.

"You have a great view. It overlooks the flower garden," Phyllis says.

I push through the doors and step out on the terrace and I'm immediately blown away. The view is amazing. There's a field of beautiful flowers that seem to go on forever. And the air, oh my gosh! The air is so fragrant. I close my eyes and take a deep inhale letting the aroma fill my nostrils and lungs and for a moment all my troubles are forgotten.

"Aaron's brought your bags up. I can put your things away for you if you like," Phyllis says from behind me.

I turn to face her. "No, that's okay. I can do it."

She smiles warmly at me. "Okay, sweetheart. I guess I'll leave you now. Dinner's at seven. I'll come grab you and take you to the dining room when it's time."

"Okay," I say.

Phyllis stares at me, the space between her eyes crinkling, her hands folded tightly in front of her belly. She looks like she wants to say something.

"Is there anything else?" I ask.

She shakes her head. "No, I'll see you in a little bit," she says then turns and leaves.

CHAPTER THREE

Phyllis shows back up at seven on the dot. "Time for dinner, Fallon," she says peeking her head in the door.

I follow her though this maze of a house to the dining room, which is, to no surprise very large and very elegant. It looks like one of those dining rooms out of *Better Homes & Garden* magazine. It's very formal. Very sleek and sophisticated. The center piece of the room is a beautiful Italian chandelier hanging over the center of a long, rectangular dining table. The navy blue upholstered chairs with a silver trellis design brings dignified color to the room.

My grandfather is already seated at the head of the table when we get there. There's a place setting to the right of him that I assume is for me. As soon as I sit down a man seemingly appears out nowhere holding a tray with two covered plates. He sits one down in front of my grandfather and removes the lid. He sits the other one in front of me, removes the lid then disappears back to wherever he came from.

I stare at the plate and my stomach grumbles. The food looks and smells delicious. It's some sort of fancy beef dish with mash potatoes and roasted carrots. I dig in and we eat in silence for a good while.

"I'm sorry about your mother," my grandfather says.

I stop chewing and look at him. He's staring at me waiting for me to respond. I swallow my food then say a quiet, "Thank you."

"What do you know about your father?" he asks.

I really don't feel like talking but I suppose it'll be rude to sit at his table and ignore him. "Not much," I say. "Just that he and my mom met when she was nineteen, they were in love and he died before I was born."

"Your father was my first and only child. Your grandmother, Patricia, couldn't have any more children after him so he was our pride and joy," he says with a smile. "He was smart and funny and great at sports. He was captain of the row team in high school and even rowed in college."

My ears perk up. I may not have much to say to this man but I want to hear what he has to say about my father.

"He had a great eye for business, your father. In fact, he was handling the Midwest operations for the family business when he met your mother. I had great plans for that boy. It was devastating when we lost him."

"How did he die?" I ask. "Mom told me he was in an accident but she never told me anymore than that."

A shadow of sadness crosses my grandfather's face. "Car accident. He was going too fast and lost control of his car."

"Oh," I say and stare down at my plate.

"Not a day goes by that I don't miss him but it's been a long time and life goes on."

"I guess…" I say.

He points at my plate. "You finished? I'd like to show you something."

"Sure," I say, looking down at my plate which is nearly clean.

"Come with me," he says getting up from the table.

I follow him out of the dining room and down a long hallway into a study. He leads me over to a table full of framed photographs.

He picks one up and hands it to me. "This is your father."

I take the picture and look at it. The man in the picture is handsome. He looks a lot like me with a head full of curly, tawny brown hair and bright emerald color eyes. Mom only had one picture of my father. It was one of them sitting at a table at the coffee shop where they met. They were both young and vibrant. My father had his arm wrapped around my mother's shoulder and my mother was nestled against him. They both wore big, happy smiles. The picture is old. Mom had it for years so it's worn and fading but you can clearly see how much they loved each other. It's one of the things I brought with me from Nebraska.

"I don't know how much you know about our family but as you can see we're very well off and had your father lived he would be in line to inherit everything." He looks at me as if he's waiting for me to say something.

I really don't know what to say so I stay quiet.

"I've wondered since his death what to do with my companies and other assets seeing I had no heir but now that you've come along the Gamble legacy can continue. You'll inherit all of this. Everything."

I nearly drop the picture. Me? Inherit everything? He's got to be kidding. "Ummm...I'm not sure that's a good idea."

"Of course, it is. You're a Gamble."

I sit the picture back on the table. "Yeah, but I didn't grow up here and I don't know anything about business or money."

"You'll learn. I've already enrolled you into one of the best private schools in the country and after high school you'll go to one of the best colleges and you'll intern with me during summer break. You'll be fine."

He's clearly got things all figured out but for me this is a bit too much. I just lost my mother for fucks sake and he's already mapped out my entire future. I guess I should be happy. How often does a bright future and a big fortune fall into a person's lap? "Thank you, Sir, but..."

"Call me grandfather," he says cutting me off. "And I know this may seem like a lot but just give it time. You'll get used to things. You're a part of the elite class now, Fallon." He sits down on the dark leather couch and motions for me to sit on the sofa across from him.

I sit down and fold my hands in my lap. I feel so small in this room. In his presence.

"I've set up some appointments with a therapist to help you deal with everything going on. Your mother's death, finding out that you have family, moving to another state. I know quick and massive changes like this can be difficult and I want to make sure you're okay. I need you in top shape. You'll see her twice a week until school starts."

I suppose it's not a bad idea to meet with a therapist. He's right after all. I've been through some heavy shit. But, does he really think I'll be fine after seeing a therapist for a few weeks? The way I feel right now, it'll take two lifetimes for me to get over my mother's death. "What happens when school starts? Do I just stop seeing the therapist?"

"I've enrolled you in Bradford Academy. It's one of the best boarding schools in the county. You'll be staying on campus during the school year and you'll see the school therapist once a week after school starts. I've vetted him out. He has an extraordinary reputation."

My eyes bug out. Boarding school? Seriously? I can feel my breath start to quicken as panic sets in. Too many changes too fast. I close my eyes and count to ten trying to calm myself down.

"Perhaps you should lay down for a bit. I'm sure this is all very overwhelming," my grandfather says. He gets up and comes over to the sofa. He grabs one of the pillows and lays it flat on the sofa then motions for me to lay down.

I lay down and curl into a fetal position. My grandfather covers me with a blanket and before long I'm fast asleep.

The next few weeks fly by. I spend most of my time in my beautifully decorated bedroom surfing the internet and talking to my friends back in Nebraska. They're all in awe of my newfound wealth. Something I still can't wrap my head around.

I've had fifteen sessions with the therapist and the pain of losing mom still hasn't gone away. In fact, it hurts just as much now as it did before. The therapist keeps telling me to give it time but it's time that's killing me. Every minute without my mom is torture. I miss her more than anything in the world and no amount of money or nice things is going to change that.

Summer's coming to a close and school starts in three days. I'm a nervous wreck. I spent the last few days researching Bradford Academy. It's literally the stomping ground of the kids of Texas high society. And when I say high society I'm talking billionaire status and I guess I'm now in that group seeing how my grandfather is worth eighty billion dollars. I'm still trying to wrap my head around that one.

There's a knock at my bedroom door. "Come in," I say.

Phyllis and the family butler, Langford, come in carrying a shitload of bags.

"We come bearing gifts," Phyllis sings and I smile.

Phyllis has been the one bright spot in this otherwise shitty time in my life. She's like the grandmother I never had. She dotes on me. Checking on me often, always giving me hugs and telling me stories about my father when he was young. Those are the times when I'm really happy; when she's talking about my father. She has so many stories. He was a handful but she loved him like he was her own.

"What's all that?" I ask pushing my laptop aside.

"It's all your stuff for school." She sits the bags down and starts pulling stuff out. "School uniforms, socks, shoes, undies, a new backpack. There's so much stuff. Your grandfather outdid himself."

I walk over and start looking through the stuff. There's a bunch of short, black plaid skirts with tiny gold stripes, a couple dozen white button downs and skinny neckties in the same pattern as the skirt. I lift up a package of socks. They're also black with tiny gold stripes at the top and their knee high. "I have to wear these?" I ask with a frown.

Phyllis lets out a small laugh. "You sure do. They take dress code seriously at that school. Your father tried to rebel against the dress code once and he almost got expelled."

"I bet grandfather didn't like that," I quip.

"Oh, your grandfather wasn't the one he had to worry about. Your grandmother gave him a good to do."

"A good to do?" I say with a frown. *What does that even mean?*

Phyllis lets out a deep, hearty laugh. "That's just something us old folks say. It just means that she gave him hell and kept him in line is all."

"Oh," I say. It's odd really but since I've been here my grandfather has only mentioned my grandmother once. I know absolutely nothing about her. "What was she like, my grandmother?"

Phyllis sighs. "She was a complicated woman. Very beautiful. Came from a good family. Appearances meant everything to her so she could be pretty hard on the family when things got out of order but she meant well. She loved your father dearly. Took it real hard when he died."

"My mom said she blamed her for my father's death."

Phyllis takes my hand in hers. "Losing your father was extremely painful for your grandmother and she lashed out a lot right after his death. But she was grieving and when we grieve we sometimes do and say things out of pain. And your grandmother was in a lot of pain."

"Yeah but if she hadn't said those things to my mother maybe I would have gotten to know my father's family sooner."

"Maybe but you're getting to know them now. Well, your grandfather, at least."

"But am I though? We've barely spoken since I've been here."

Phyllis tucks a stray curl behind my ear and smiles warmly at me. "Your grandfather is doing the best he can. It was a shock, him finding out about you. You look so much like your father. It's just as hard for him to adjust to things as it is for you but I know he's happy you're here, Fallon. You two just need time."

We sit quietly for a few minutes. Me digesting what she said and her allowing me the time to do so.

"I'm so nervous about starting school on Monday. It sucks

being the new kid," I say.

"You'll be fine. You're a good kid. Smart. Pretty. Those kids will take to you real quick. You'll have a lot of friends in no time."

"I guess," I say, doubt shaking the lightness of my voice.

"Well at least you'll look good," Phyllis laughs grabbing some more clothes out of the bags. She holds up some designer jeans and tops.

"He didn't pick out this stuff by himself, did he?"

"Oh, child, no. Your grandfather wouldn't know where to begin shopping for a teenage girl. He hired someone. A lovely young woman who does personal shopping for a lot of the wealthy folks around here."

I hold up a pair of designer black skinny jeans with rips in all the right places and a pair of Saint Laurent, leather slip on espadrilles. "Well she has amazing taste."

Phyllis and I go through the rest of the bags. There's so many designer shoes, clothes and bags. It surreal. My wardrobe has always been decent. We couldn't afford a full wardrobe of designer clothes but Mom bought me a few pieces here and there. The few items of clothing I brought with me from Nebraska are nothing like the designer digs strewn across my bed but they're mine. They remind me of home and I'm taking them to Bradford with me too.

Langford enters the room with a large designer trunk and a couple of designer suitcases.

"Just sit them there, Langford," Phyllis instructs.

"Is that what I'm taking my stuff to Bradford in?" I ask pointing to the designer trunk and suitcases.

"Yep, now let's get to packing. There is a lot of stuff here," Phyllis says and starts folding my new clothes neatly and stacking them on the bed.

I help her and before you know it all the clothes and shoes are nicely packed in the trunk and the suitcases.

"Well that's all the clothes and shoes. Is there anything else in here you want to take?" Phyllis asks.

"Maybe the comforter set and the computer," I say looking

around the room.

"Oh no, honey, you'll have a new comforter already in your room and your grandfather got you a new laptop and iPad for school so you can leave that computer here."

"Guess he's thought of everything," I whisper.

"He's very thorough," Phyllis says with a laugh. "But seriously, he really wants to make sure you have everything you need."

I stare at the trunk and bags full of clothes and shoes sitting by the door. "I have way more than I need," I say to Phyllis.

She smiles and lets out an amused chuckle. "Oh, a lady can never have enough clothes. Now, let's go see if dinner's ready," Phyllis says moving towards the door.

We make our way to the dining room which is already set with two place settings. My grandfather enters the room a few seconds after Phyllis and I do.

"Good evening, Phyllis. Fallon," he says nodding to me.

"Good evening Mr. G. How was your day?" Phyllis asks.

"Very busy. Lots of meetings," he says walking over to his place at the table and sitting down.

"It was a busy day for us too. We got Fallon all packed and ready to go for school," she says.

"Very good," he says.

"I'll just go check on dinner," Phyllis says leaving me standing alone and staring awkwardly at my grandfather.

"Have a seat," he says, motioning to the chair across from him.

I sit down and stare nervously across the table at him.

"I know we haven't spent that much time together since you've been here but I felt it was important to give you space. I did check in with the therapist and she said your sessions were really good."

I nod my head. I still haven't really figured out how to talk to this man. He's larger than life with the big house, fancy car and all the money. And he's so distinguished. Everything about him, from the way he dresses, to the way he speaks and the way he carries himself. There's this heir of importance about him that's really intimidating.

Langford brings in our dinner. Of course, it looks and smells amazing. I dig right in.

"So, you start Bradford tomorrow," Grandfather says.

I nod.

"Bradford's a very good school. Almost a hundred percent of the students go on to Ivy League colleges. I got a look at your transcripts from your old school. You're a smart girl, Fallon. It seems you're particularly good at art," he adds.

"Thank you," I say.

"Bradford has a very robust art program. There's plenty of classes you can take as electives."

"That's nice."

He reaches into his pocket and pulls out his wallet. I watch as he pulls out a credit card and slides it across the table.

"That's for you," he says.

I pick it up. It's a black American Express Card. "Are you serious?" I gasp.

"Very. You'll be living at the academy all year and you need spending money. I was going to get you a car but I wasn't sure if you'd gotten your license yet."

"Just my permit. Mom was teaching me how to drive before she got sick. I mean, I know how to drive. We just never got around to going to the DMV so I could take the test."

"Well we can get that taken care of. I figure we get you settled at the academy first and then we can get you your license sometime down the road."

"Okay," I nod.

We both go back to eating, neither of us saying anything for a few minutes.

"Fallon."

"Yes," I say looking up.

"I know you'll do well at Bradford. Even though you didn't grow up the same way the kids that go there did, you're a Gamble. You come from very good stock. You come from a family that is very wealthy, very prominent and holds a lot of power. It's important that you uphold the Gamble family name."

"Okay," I say not really knowing what he means by that.
"Very good," he says and goes back to eating his meal.

CHAPTER FOUR

Monday rolls around quickly and before I know it I find myself standing outside the bottom of the wide, worn steps of Bradford Academy. My grandfather drove me, or should I say, Aaron drove us to the school and before I got out of the car grandfather told me to make him proud. No pressure or anything.

So here I stand in my freshly pressed uniform, fingers wrapped tight and strangling the strap of my backpack too scared to move.

Kids move past me barely giving me a second glance. The screech of tires against pavement draws my attention to the parking lot and I look over to see a metallic purple Aston Martin whip into one of the empty parking spaces. It's got to be the most beautiful car I've ever seen. I've only seen Aston Martins in music videos, never in real life. It's quite a sight to behold. I stare wide-eyed and mouth open as the doors lift up to the heavens and out step two of the most beautiful boys I've ever seen in my entire life. The one climbing out of the passenger side is the epitome of perfection with flawless mahogany skin, a perfectly chiseled jaw, full lips and the body of an athlete. I can hardly take my eyes off him. There's just something about him. A certain swag. Whatever it is, it's got my blood pumping.

He looks over to the boy getting out of the driver's side. I follow his gaze and my heart flip-flops. The boy's almost too good to look at with his thick mop of flaxen colored hair falling strategically around his face. He's dressed in the boy's school uniform of khaki pants, white button down and tie; only the top few buttons on his shirt are undone and his tie hangs loosely around his neck giving him that effortless disheveled but gorgeous look.

Heat rushes through my body and I'm suddenly very hot. I have the urge to loosen my tie and roll down my knee knocks.

Pretty boy with the perfect skin and full lips says something to the flaxen-haired Adonis and that lovely mouth of his splits into a smirk, one that's dark; almost menacing. Suddenly he turns and looks at me as if he can feel me watching him. Our gazes clash and that smirk grows a bit more menacing as he lifts a curious brow. It's like he's baiting me. It's unnerving but I don't look away. He's too captivating a creature not to look at.

Our silent game is broken when a gorgeous blonde with a perfect tan and legs for days throws herself into him. He catches her, slinging an arm around her waist and pressing her tight against his body. She giggles and presses her mouth to his. The whole time his eyes are still locked with mine.

An irrational bout of jealousy fills my body and I press my lips into a firm line before finally turning away and bounding up the steps into the front entrance of the school building.

"Not the best way to start the year, Fallon," I mumble as I clutch the paper detailing the agenda for my first day. I'm supposed to report to student orientation, wherever that is.

I wonder around the halls for a good ten minutes before a stunning Indian girl with dark hair and dark eyes comes up to me.

"Fallon Gamble?" she asks her mouth splitting into a friendly smile.

"Uh, yeah," I say, wondering how she knows my name.

"Oh good. I've been looking for you. I'm Devya Nadar," she says holding out her hand.

"Hi," I say taking her hand.

"I've been assigned to show you around campus. The school always assigns someone to the newbies. Although the newbies are usually freshman. We don't get many transfers at Bradford, especially juniors," she adds.

"Guess I'm the lucky exception," I say.

She giggles. "Funny. You've got a sense of humor. That's good.

You're going to need it around here. Things can get a little intense at Bradford and humor helps."

"I'll keep that in mind," I say shifting my book bag to my other shoulder.

A bell chimes and Devya starts. "Shoot! We gotta go. Orientation is about to start and we cannot be late," she says grabbing my arm and pulling me down the hall.

We race down several hallways and across a courtyard before barreling through a set of double-doors leading to the auditorium which is already filled with students. Devya pulls me along with her towards the front of the room were there's a stage with a podium set up.

"There's some empty seats over there," I say pointing to a row near the back of the room.

"Unh-unh," she says pulling me forward. "We sit up front."

"What? Why? I'm fine in the back." I protest.

Devya whips around and leans in close. "No, you're not. You're a newbie. Fresh meat. You wanna make it here, you carve out your territory from jump. The who's who of Bradford sit in the front row at assemblies. Now c'mon, you're sitting up front with me." And with that she whips back around, her long, luxurious, onyx colored hair floating softly behind her.

I notice a few students staring at me. I put my head down and quickly follow behind her.

Devya makes her way to the very front row which is full to capacity.

"No open seats. Let's just go to the back," I say and turn to head towards the back of the room. I'm stopped cold as my body slams into rock solid muscle.

"My bad," I mumble as I look up and connect with the most arresting blue-violet eyes I've ever seen.

Those blue-violet eyes narrow and take me in from head to toe and back up again. Chills run down my spine as I stare at the boy they belong to. His features are perfect in a dangerously handsome sort of way. His hair, perfectly wavy and the color of midnight falls precariously across his forehead. His lips are full, pink and totally kissable and his smell. Oh gawd! He smells of black licorice and cola. I'm not sure what it is about that combination but it's intoxicating. I reach for the edge of the seat at the end of the row to steady myself and keep from swooning. *What the hell is wrong with me?* This is the third time this morning that the sight of some boy has me all hot and bothered.

"Watch the kicks, clown," blue-violet eyes says, that pretty mouth of his turning up into a fearsome sneer.

Geez, this kid's rude as fuck but his voice is this husky purr that gets under the skin in the best possible way.

My cheeks heat and turn red. Kids nearby laugh. I'm on the verge of ducking out of there when Devya steps in, hand on hip, her glossy lips pursed.

"You all can shut the hell up before I banish you to the back of the room with the rest of the scum," she sneers at those laughing. They immediately clam up and face forward.

She turns those dark, sultry eyes on pretty boy with the sweet licorice smell. "Zade, those kicks are pretty fire but please don't be rude to my friend."

Zade cocks his eyebrow in my direction. "You taking in strays again, Devya?" He says shaking his head in disapproval.

Devya doesn't respond to his comment. Instead she smiles sweetly at him. "This is my friend Fallon. She just transferred here. She's a junior like us." She looks at me then back at Zade. "And yeah, she's my friend."

"Whatever," Zade says rolling his eyes. He moves pasts us and looks down the front row. "Move," he says pointing to three students sitting at the end of the row. They scramble immediately, grabbing their book bags and rushing to find other seats.

Zade takes the first seat. Devya sits next to him and pulls me down into the seat next to her.

A middle-aged man with dark brown hair takes the stage. He's dressed neatly in slacks, a button down and a sports coat. He wears an heir of authority but it seems forced. Just as forced as the practiced smile he plasters on his face. "Welcome students to another year at Bradford Academy. I'm Headmaster Dieter

Cromwell. Here at Bradford we pride ourselves on excellence in everything we do. Only the best and the brightest are privileged enough to attend our school."

"Don't forget the richest," a boy calls out from behind me and the auditorium erupts in laughter.

I turn to see who the heckler is and my heart stops. Coming up the aisle is pretty boy with the perfect mahogany skin and his flaxen haired, disarmingly beautiful friend that I saw in the parking lot this morning. They're heading straight towards us and the closer they get the more nervous I become, but they pass right by me as if I'm not even there.

"Ya'll know the drill," Pretty Boy says and flicks his thumb at the two boys sitting next to Zade. "Give them seats up."

"Yeah, of course. No problem, Lucca." one of the boys says and jumps up. "C'mon, he says to the kid sitting next to him. That kid gets up without a word and they both head to the back of the auditorium to find other seats.

"What's up Zade, man?" Lucca says, dapping him up.

"Sup' Lucca." He says, dapping up Mr. Beautiful before turning to the other Adonis. "Sup, Alisander."

"Chillin'," Alisander says as he sits down.

"If you boys are done, we can get back to orientation," Headmaster Cromwell says from the podium.

"Chill out, Cromwell. You give the same speech every year. It's not like we're hearing anything new," Alisander says.

"Real talk," Lucca chimes in.

Snickers can be heard throughout the auditorium.

"All right that's enough. Anymore from you boys and you'll earn your first demerit before we reach first period."

"Whatever," the boys mumble at the same time.

"As I was saying, we pride ourselves on excellence and I expect nothing but the best from all of you this year. Our students stand out for their desire and drive for knowledge, their passion, creativity and their commitment to service. Over the past one hundred and fifty years we've had the privilege of knowing and nurturing over twenty thousand graduates who've made us very proud," Headmaster Cromwell continues. He then goes on about the long-standing history and traditions of the school and what he expects from us.

I'm trying to pay attention to what he's saying but my focus keeps getting drawn to the three boys sitting just a few feet away from me - Lucca, Alisander and Zade. First of all, those names sound like something from Greek Mythology. Very otherworldly. Very much how the boys look. They could all be models, those three. Lucca with his sculpted face, flawless skin and muscular physic. Alisander with that lustrous, flaxen hair and beautiful mouth. I die! And let's not forget Zade. Zade, the dark and dangerous one with the all-consuming blue-violet eyes and intoxicating black licorice and cola scent. I'm shook. They don't make boys like this in Nebraska.

"Fallon," Devya says. She's standing over me. In fact, the entire front row is standing up and clearing out.

I look up to see that Headmaster Cromwell is leaving the stage and students are filing out of the auditorium. Seems I missed the rest of Headmaster Cromwell's speech because I was too busy drooling over the magnificent three.

"Is the new girl simple or something?" Alisander asks and every kid within earshot laughs. "Hey, new girl. Are you simple?" He asks cocking his head at me.

"Her name is Fallon," Devya says.

"Yeah, that's Fallon. Devya's new stray," Zade says, his blue-violet eyes sparking with menace.

"Be nice, Zade" Devya says, her voice sugary sweet.

Zade gives her a noncommittal stare.

"Ooh, just wait 'til the girls find out you're collecting strays again, Devya. They're gonna eat this one alive just like the last one." Lucca says shaking his head.

"Yeah, let's see how long she lasts," Alisander adds.

"Probably not long. Once Bexley gets a hold of her she's done," Lucca adds.

"Too bad," Zade chimes in looking me up and down. He's got this sort of half grin on his face but there's nothing cute or sweet about it at all. Actually, it's a little scary. There's something dangerous about him. He's definitely the boy parents warn their teenage daughters about. "She's kind of cute," he says.

"Yeah, cute enough to fuck one good time then toss," Alisander says.

The other boys break out in laughter and push past me.

I've never been more embarrassed in my life. I've dealt with some jerky boys before but they were nothing like these three. Matter of fact, I've never met any boys like Lucca, Alisander or Zade. These three are all cock and bull. They're rich and good looking and they know it. They say what they want and they do what they want. They carry their authority around like a hammer smashing all inferior beings in their way. Me included.

"Don't worry about them, Fallon," Devya says. "They can be complete asses sometimes but they're cool."

Did she not just hear what they said to me? Zade called me a stray not once but twice and Alisander made some crude joke about fucking me and tossing me aside. But they're cool. *Yeah. Okay.*

"We should get to first period before the bell rings," Devya says looping her arm through mine and pulling me towards the exit. "There are three paths leading from the auditorium," Devya starts as we step outside. She points to her left. "That path leads to student housing. The path on the right leads to the administration building and the parking lot and this path here, the one we're walking on, leads to the courtyard that feeds into the main building where all the classes are held."

We make our way across the courtyard which, by the way, is way fancier than the courtyard at my old school. This one reminds me of the courtyards you find at a fancy hotel. There's several sitting areas strategically placed throughout the courtyard. They're all set up conversational style with each sitting area having a coffee table as the center piece and the loveseats and armchairs are placed around the table for easy group gatherings. I have no idea what the furniture is made of but it's a lovely sky blue and grey color and it looks expensive.

"We normally hang out in the courtyard in between classes.

Some of the school fundraisers are held out here," Devya explains.

This is all good to know but my mind keeps wandering back to what Alisander said earlier about the girls eating me alive especially this Bexley chic. He made it a point to mention her by name so she's clearly the one I need to worry about. "Who's Bexley?" I ask.

Devya lets out a wary sigh. "Bexley Barringer, she's the Queen Bee around here. She's blonde, beautiful and stings like a viper. Just try not to get on her bad side. Her family donated like half the buildings on this campus so she gets away with a lot here."

"I'll do my best," I say with a frown. "So, what did Lucca mean when he said the girls are gonna eat me alive just like the last one? Was there another new girl? Did they do something to her?"

"It's kind of a long story and we don't have much time so I'll tell you about it later, okay," Devya says looking away.

"Alright," I say, making a mental note to ask her about it again later.

"So, what dorm are you in?" Devya asks, changing the subject.

"Barringer Hall," I say. Oddly enough I haven't even seen my dorm room yet. My grandfather sent his people to set everything up for me. I'll be seeing it for the first time after classes finish for the day.

Worry flashes across Devya's face but only for a second before she plasters a smile back on her face. "I'm in Amherst. The Queen Bee and most of her clique is in Barringer."

"Should I be worried?" I ask feeling deep down that I should.

"Ummm…no…I mean, you haven't even had your first run-in with the girls yet. Maybe they'll like you right away and then there's nothing to worry about," she says.

That was such a non-answer. I start to panic a bit. "So, I should be worried?"

Devya opens the door to the main building. "Not yet. For now, let's just worry about getting to first period on time. What do you have first period?"

I'm clearly not going to get a straight answer out of her where Bexley and her click are concerned so I pull my schedule out of my backpack. "Chemistry," I say.

"Darn. I have history first period. I tell you what, I'll walk you to first period to make sure you get there on time. This place can feel like a maze to new people," she says and leads the way to my chemistry class.

While Devya's chattering on about her class schedule as we walk, I take in the magnificence of the school. The inside of Bradford Academy is the perfect mix of modernity and old school charm with its hardwood floors, large bay windows and crown molding all setting the foundation for the eclectic and bright colored paintings that line the walls and the modern amenities available to the students and staff. It's really a beautiful school. I can't help but be impressed.

We reach room three fifty-seven where my chemistry class is located and Devya disentangles herself from my arm and faces me. "Well, this is it. Your first period class. I'll meet you right here after class. We both have Professor Cluzet next period for French so we can walk to class together."

"Okay," I nod but don't make a move to go into the classroom.

Devya puts her hand on my shoulder. "Don't be nervous. You'll be fine," she says then turns and walks away.

"I hope so," I mumble then walk into my first period class. I keep my eyes trained forward doing my best not to look at anyone as I make my way to the back of the classroom and sit down at one of the lab tables. People at this school seem to have a thing about the front row and the last thing I want is to be humiliated and made to find another seat.

Students file into the classroom and so far, there's no sign of the magnificent three which makes me breathe a bit easier. I can't seem to focus when those three are around.

I pull out the new tablet my grandfather bought me and log into the school's online learning system and check into class as instructed in the syllabus then wait for the teacher to arrive.

Just when I start to relax, in walks Zade with a beautiful caramel skinned girl draped all over him. And when I say beautiful, I mean beautiful. I'm talking large, brown doe eyes, cute heart shaped face, pouty lips, and a make-up job to die for. Her make-up game is straight out of one those beauty blogger videos on YouTube. She's wearing the standard Bradford Academy uniform but on her the short, pleated skirt, knee high socks and white button down looks absolutely salacious. She looks like total jail bait.

Following closely behind Zade and the beautiful, caramel skinned siren are two other equally beautiful girls. One's a brunette with long, lustrous locks that frame an angelic face. Her pert little nose and plump lips are in perfect symmetry with each other and her ice blue eyes are shrouded in long thick lashes. In a word, she's perfect.

Walking next to her is a brown-skinned beauty that looks really similar, if not exactly, like the girl draped across Zade. They have to be twins.

The four of them make their way to the back of the classroom and I immediately get nervous. I look down at my tablet pretending to be engrossed in whatever's on there.

"Well, look who we have here. It's Devya's stray," Zade says and I cringe.

Of course, he would notice me and of course the attention he paid wouldn't be nice. I look up from my tablet. "Hello. Zade, is it?" I say, pretending not to remember who he is.

He doesn't reply. Instead he turns to the three girls who are already staring at me with disdain. "Girls, I don't think you've met the new girl. This is Devya's stray." He turns to me. "Stray, meet the girls. This is Indigo, Tatum and Chloe," he says motioning to each girl.

I look at each of them; Indigo, the caramel beauty he walked in with, Tatum, the other brown beauty and obvious twin of Indigo and Chloe, the gorgeous brunette with the angelic face. All three are extremely attractive and currently shooting daggers at me. Clearly these are the girls that Alisander was referring to. At least a few of them.

"So why is Devya's stray sitting in the back? Shouldn't she be up front with the rest of the losers?" Indigo says to Zade, a deep scowl marring her pretty features.

Zade shrugs. "I guess Devya hasn't taught her the rules yet."

Tatum moves close to the lab table I'm sitting at. "Move, Stray. This lab table belongs to me and Chloe," she says, her tone high and mighty.

I look from her to Chloe to Indigo then at Zade. All four of them are looking at me like I'm gum on the bottom to their shoe. Not to mention some of the other students in class have turned around and are watching us.

I have a choice to make here. I can get up and move or stand my ground and tell them to fuck off. Everything in me wants to do the latter but something tells me that would open a whole can of worms that I don't need right now. The first day of school has barely begun. I really don't want any drama on day one so I quietly pick up my things and move to an empty seat at one of the other tables. I can hear Zade and his bevy of cruel beauties laughing as I walk away.

CHAPTER FIVE

As planned I wait for Devya outside the classroom. I had to endure hard shoulder brushes from Indigo, Tatum and Chloe on their way out. Zade just ignored me which really kind of bothered. And I know that is insane seeing how he's been an unmitigated ass to me from jump. But I don't know, there's just something about him. Something dark. Maybe even dangerous. And those blue-violet eyes, they do something to me.

"How was first period," Devya says all cheery as she walks up to me.

"I met some of the girls," I say.

Worry clouds Devya's face. "How'd it go?"

"Well, let's see. They kicked me out of my seat and called me a stray."

"So, no bloodshed. Not bad," Devya says and starts walking down the hall.

I run and catch up with her. "What do you mean no bloodshed?"

"I just mean that your first encounter went pretty well if all you got was booted out of your seat. Honestly, I'm surprised that's all Bexley did," she finishes.

"Bexley wasn't there," I say.

Devya stops in her tracks and turns to face me. "She wasn't? Then which girls did you meet?"

"Indigo, Tatum, and Chloe," I say.

Devya starts walking again and I fall in step with her. "Okay. Indigo can be a real bitch but Tatum and Chloe are aren't all that bad. I bet they've already told Bexley about you though," she says that last part more to herself than me. "Let me see your schedule again," she says holding her hand out.

I hand my schedule to her and watch as she looks it over, mumbling to herself the entire time.

"Good news is that your next three classes are with me. Then you have art then gym which I'm not in. Hopefully Bexley's not in your sixth or seventh period classes," she says handing my schedule back to me.

All this talk about Bexley has got me completely on edge. I'm terrified of the girl and I've yet to lay to eyes on her.

"C'mon," Devya says grabbing my arm and pulling me into second period English class. Unlike chemistry class, this room has the usual classroom setup of rows of individual desks. We go all the way to the back of the room and sit down.

"Are you sure we should be sitting back here," I ask worrying my bottom lip.

"Of course," she says looking at me like I'm crazy.

"Correction, should I be sitting back here? I've already been humiliated more than enough times to count today," I say.

Devya tosses her hair over her shoulder and squares her eyes at me. "You're a Gamble and you're with me. I belong here in the back row which means that you do too," she says then faces forward in her seat.

I sigh and pull out my tablet and check in for class before looking around wearily for any one of the girls from last period. No signs of the girls and every seat in the classroom is full except for the seat in the back row next to me. I just might get lucky and actually have a class where I don't have to deal with the girls or any of the magnificent three.

"Bonjour! Good morning class." A tall, slender woman with blonde hair and model good looks says as she enters the classroom. "I'm Madame Cluzet and I'll be your French III teacher this year," she says in a thick, French accent. "Since it's the start of a new year, I'd like for everyone to introduce themselves. En Français," she adds. "We'll start with you," she says pointing to a redhead in the first row.

The girl stands up and is about to speak when the classroom door swings open and in saunters Alisander, a cocky grin on his face.

"Monsieur Davenport, gentil de vous joindre à nous," Professor Cluzet says.

"Oui, Oui, professor," Alisander says and the class erupts in laughter.

"Two years of French and a tutor and you've still learned nothing. Very disappointing, Alisander. Please have a seat," she says gesturing towards the back of the classroom.

Crap. The only open seat is the one next to me. I try not to watch as Alisander makes his way down the aisle. But it's hard not to look at him. He's so damn beautiful. And the way he moves. He has a real relaxed, almost lazy gait as if time doesn't exist or matter to him.

"You again," he says cocking an eyebrow at me as he sits down.

"Monsieur Davenport, silence! S'il vous plait," Professor Cluzet says. "You'll get your chance to introduce yourself just like everyone else."

The student introductions go quickly and before I know it, it's my turn. Panic wells up in my throat and my stomach knots in fear.

Professor Cluzet looks at me expectantly, a pleasant smile on her face.

I slowly stand, my eyes on Professor Cluzet. I'm far too nervous to look at anyone else. Besides so far, I've gotten nothing but shit from every student I've encountered. Well, except for Devya.

"Bonjour," I start, my voice a bit shaky. Introducing myself in French should be a piece of cake. I absolutely love the language and the culture. Back home in Nebraska I had the highest grade in my French class and was in the French National Honor Society. But things are different here. While I sat in class reading and reciting French from textbooks I'm sure these kids were probably lounging somewhere on the French Riviera experiencing the culture in real life.

Professor Cluzet smiles encouragingly at me.

"Je m'appelle Fallon Gamble. Je viens d'arriver de Nebraska," I say and quickly sit back down.

"It's very nice to have you, Mademoiselle Gamble. Your enunciation is parfaite. Good job." She looks at Alisander. "Monsieur Davenport, you're up."

"Nah, I'm good. Everybody already knows who I am."

Professor Cluzet looks like she wants to say something but instead takes a deep breath and moves on with class.

"Yo, Devya," Alisander whispers leaning in my direction but completely ignoring the fact that I'm sitting in the seat between him and Devya.

"What's up?" Devya whispers.

"Friday night. First party of the year at my family's New Braunfels house on the river."

"Ugh! I love that house. I'm so there." She looks at me. "Alisander throws the best parties and his family's river house is sick. Wait 'til you see it."

"No strays allowed, Devya," Alisander says, his face marked with loathing.

"Oh c'mon, Alisander. Fallon's cool. You just need to get to know her," Devya says.

"All I need to know is that she's not one of us," he says, his lips twisting into a cynical smile.

Devya narrows her eyes at him. "Seriously! You do know who her grandfather is, right?"

"Yeah, so," Alisander says with a shrug.

So, her family has the highest net worth of anyone at this school," she says.

"Again, so what. She didn't grow up with all that money or the lifestyle. She has no idea how things work in our circle. She's not one of us. The girls will never accept her and you know it. But if you want to put her through the same shit that Ruby Stratton went through last year then that's on you," he sneers.

I watch quietly as they discuss me as if I'm not even there. Maybe I don't want to go to the stupid party. And maybe I didn't grow up with money or the lifestyle these kids had but I had a good life back in Nebraska. My mom worked hard to give me everything I needed and more.

My heart constricts at the thought of my mother. It's been such a shit day with me dealing with these entitled brats and worrying about this Bexley girl that I have yet to encounter, that I haven't thought about my mom once. I don't know if that's a good or bad thing.

"Ruby Stratton was different. That entire situation was different so don't go there," Devya says to Alisander, her face serious.

"Whatever. Bring her if you want but she's your responsibility," he says and leans back in his chair.

"Goody!" Devya exclaims smiling big at me. "We're going to have so much fun."

I make it through third and fourth period with no incidents. None of the girls or the magnificent three are in either of those periods so I'm able to relax. None of the other students in class paid me any mind. They basically just ignored me which was fine with me.

After fourth period Devya and I head to the dining hall for lunch. Now, this isn't your run of the mill school cafeteria. The dining hall at Bradford Academy is something like a five-star restaurant. As soon as we walk in I notice the beautifully polished hardwood floor and contrasting walls in a soft cream color. Elegant chandeliers hang from the ceiling throughout the room and the dining tables are made of thick, dark mahogany wood with lovely floral carvings running along the edges of the table and along the base. The chairs are the same beautiful dark mahogany with high backs and the same floral design runs along the back of the tops of the chairs.

I follow Devya to an empty table located in the center of the room. The table is set with twelve place settings of stark white dinnerware with gold trimming. There's a menu sitting in the middle of each plate.

I take a seat next to Devya and pick up the menu. There are four entrée options; grilled salmon with garlic and herbs, roasted chicken, roast beef tenderloin with a wine sauce and vegetarian lasagna. There's a plethora of side dish choices like roasted potatoes, sautéed spinach, green beans, herb rice and more. There's even a dessert option of a mini lemon mousse strawberry cake or a dark chocolate mignon cake.

"Is this for real," I ask looking at Devya.

"What do you mean," she replies looking at her menu.

I wave the menu at her. "This is a real life menu with gourmet style dishes. Lunch at my old school mostly consisted of stale pizza and cold fries."

"Well, you're not in Kansas anymore, Dorothy," she says with a smile.

"Nebraska," I say.

"What?" She says frowning at me.

"I was making a joke that clearly wasn't funny so never mind."

A man who looks to be in his mid-thirties appears at our table. He's dressed neatly in black slacks, a white button down and a black vest. He's holding a tablet in his hand. "Good afternoon, ladies. What may I get for you?" He asks.

"I'll have the salmon, sautéed spinach and herb rice," Devya says her eyes still on the menu in her hand.

"Very good," the man says then looks at me. "And for you?"

They have freaking waiters taking lunch orders? This is crazy.

"Miss?" The man says, his face neutral as he waits for me to answer.

"Ummm, I'll have the roasted chicken, potatoes and green beans," I say.

"Very good," he says and takes our menus and disappears.

"So, you're taking art," Devya says fixing her gaze on me.

"Yeah," I nod.

"So, are you a painter or sculptor or do you just like to draw?"

"I paint," I say. My chest tightens thinking about the last time I held a paint brush. It was before mom got really sick. I sort of stopped painting after she went into the hospital. I didn't even bring my art supplies with me to Texas. I suppose Shannon boxed them up and put them in storage.

"That's cool," Devya says. "I love artists. They're so…"

"They're so what?" Zade says walking up to the table and sitting down. His black licorice and cola scent wafts over to me and I try not to be affected by it.

"Interesting," Devya finishes. "Anybody who can create something beautiful out of a blank canvas is just so interesting to me." Devya says.

"If you say so," Zade says, his generous mouth tipping up at the corners.

"Oh c'mon, Zade. You know what I mean. Being that you're a pretty bad ass painter." Devya looks over at me. "Fallon's an artist too. She's a painter like you."

"I dabble a little," I say, color filling my cheeks. Nobody asked Devya to share that little tidbit about me. I feel like the less these people know about me the better chances I have of making it through this year with as little damage as possible.

I chance a glance over at Zade. Blue-violet eyes watch me curiously across the surface of the fancy dining table. A warm shiver races down my spine. I'm somewhere between being unnerved and aroused and it's confusing as hell.

Our waiter appears at the table with me and Devya's food. He takes Zade's order before disappearing again.

"Zade, you piece of shit! Why didn't you wait for us in the courtyard," Alisander yells as he enters the dining hall followed by Lucca and a group of girls. Three of whom I recognize very well. Indigo, Tatum and Chloe from first period and there are two more girls with them now. Two stunningly gorgeous girls. Both blonde and one I recognize from the parking lot earlier this morning. It's the girl who threw herself at Alisander. I thought she was pretty from far away but up close her beauty is almost blinding. She's a total bombshell. She's thin with legs for days and has this perfectly symmetrical face with a thin straight nose and full pouty lips. Her eyes are this amazing aqua blue and to top it off she has this thick, glossy mane of blonde hair that falls perfectly around her face, shoulders and down her back. Not to mention how perfectly her make-up is done.

The other blonde is just as beautiful but with a lot more edge. Her hair is more of a platinum blonde that's shaved on the sides and the top is gelled and styled in a super edgy, super cute way. Everything about her screams rebel from the hair to the dark way she's painted her eyes to the haphazard way she wears her uniform. Her skirt is rolled up making it shorter than most, her tie hangs loose around her neck and she's wearing thigh high socks instead of the knee high ones the rest of us are wearing. She looks like a total rock star. It really is insane how attractive everyone in this school is.

"Crap," Devya says, the word barely audible.

I shoot her a look and for the first time all day she actually looks a bit nervous. "What?" I ask.

"Bexley," is all she says.

Clearly, she's referring to one of the blondes. Which one, I'm not sure.

The seven of them make their way to our table. Lucca and Alisander take a seat but the girls remain standing.

"So, you're the stray I've been hearing about," the bombshell says a nasty sneer gracing her pretty mouth.

"Here we go," Alisander says, leaning back in his chair.

"Hey Bexley, this is-" Devya starts to introduce me but Bexley holds up a finger shushing her before she can even get my name out.

"Wasn't talking to you, Devya darling," she says her steely gaze fixed on me.

My hands curl into fist and press into my thighs as I brace myself for whatever vitriol Bexley is about to reign on me.

"You're even more homely looking than Tatum said," she laughs and the group of hens standing with her join in.

"You must be Bexley," I say.

"I am," she says. She leans over the table, pointing a manicured finger at me. "And you, stray bitch, are sitting at the wrong table.

You see, this here table belongs to us," she gestures towards everyone else at the table. "Bradford's cream of the crop, top of the food chain, the pure bloods and some accidental transplant from bumfuck Nebraska is not welcome at this table."

A shudder of embarrassment races through me as more kids enter the dining hall and watch Bexley's verbal assault on me. This entire day has been one humiliation after another at the hands of these entitled assholes and I've reached the end of my rope. "If you don't want to sit here, there are plenty of other tables in this dining hall. Pick one," I clap back at her.

"You trashy, little, stray bitch. Do you have any idea who I am? I will make your life a living hell," Bexley grits out.

"Is everything alright over here?" Professor Cluzet says, making her way over to our table.

"Everything's fine. Bexley was just introducing herself," I say with a smirk.

Professor Cluzet looks from me to Bexley clearly not believing a word I said.

"Yeah, I was just welcoming her to Bradford. It should be a bang-up year for her," Bexley says, her aqua eyes narrowing as she looks at me. "C'mon girls, let's eat in the courtyard today."

"But I wanted to eat with Zade," Indigo pouts.

Bexley whips her head, turning her nasty gaze on Indigo. "Seriously? Let's go," she says, spinning around and heading for the door.

"I think I'll stay inside and eat," edgy blonde says sitting down.

Bexley halts and turns back towards the table. "Whatever, Harlyn." She trains her eyes on me. "Watch your back, Stray." she says and with a flip of her hair she turns around and heads out the door, her minions in tow.

"You really should heed her warning. Bex can be vicious. I'm Harlyn…Radcliffe," edgy blonde says, leaning back in her chair and kicking her foot up on the table.

"I'm Fallon," I say.

"Yeah, I know. Everybody knows who you are. Illegitimate granddaughter of Wilson Gamble, grew up poor with your mom in Nebraska, she died and your grandfather took you in. That pretty much sum it up?"

"I guess, but we weren't exactly poor. More like middle class," I say.

"Poor," everyone at the table, including Devya, says.

"I guess compared to how you guys grew up I would be classified as poor but my mom provided pretty well for us. I had everything I needed and I never went hungry."

They all just look at me like I'm speaking a language they don't understand.

"Whatever," Harlyn says as if she's grown bored of the conversation. She tosses her gaze to Alisander. "First party of the year is at your family's river house I hear."

"Yep! It's gonna be lit too. You know how I do," Alisander says, his mouth turned up into a cocky ass grin.

"You inviting any freshman? I saw a couple of real cuties in this new class," Lucca says.

"Oh, hell yeah! All hot girls are welcome," Alisander says spreading his arms wide in invitation.

"What about you, Stray? You coming to the party?" Harlyn asks looking back at me, her grey eyes assessing.

"The names Fallon," I reply.

"Yeah, about that. You're known as The Stray around here so you might as well get used to it," she says matter-of-factly. "So, are you coming to the party or not?"

Alisander chimes in before I can respond. "So, are you saying that the stray is hot, Harlyn?" Alisander asks, a teasing smile on his face.

Harlyn cocks her head to the side studying me. "She's a little plain looking for me but nothing a good make-over couldn't fix. I mean look at her. That skin is flawless. All tan and dewy, not a blemish in sight. And don't act like you didn't notice those gorgeous green eyes and that nice little pouty mouth of hers. I can't really see the body because she's sitting down but on first assessment, definitely a hottie hiding under all that boring," she says swirling her finger at me.

"You're such a lesbian, Harlyn. I love it!" Alisander jokes.

"I'm bi you ass," Harlyn spits.

"Whatever. You like eating pussy and I love that about you," Alisander laughs.

"Right!" Lucca chimes in and the two fist pound.

"You guys are so crude," Devya says shaking her head.

Through this entire exchange, I notice that Zade hasn't said a word. He's just been sitting back watching us through hooded eyes, that gorgeous face of his is a perfect mask. It makes me want to know him. Know what he's thinking. Know what he likes and what he doesn't. Know what makes him tick.

"This is so exciting," Devya says, her dark eyes shining. "We're totally giving you a make-over before the party, Fallon"

"Ummm, that's okay. I'm good." I protest.

"You'll help, won't you, Harlyn," Devya says ignoring me and looking at Harlyn.

"Sure, whatever," she responds.

"Goody! Harlyn's an artist too and her make-up skills are sick. You're gonna look so fire when we're done with you," Devya says, a shit eating grin on her face.

CHAPTER SIX

Only two more periods to go before I can finally retreat to my dorm room which I still haven't seen yet. Both Zade and Harlyn are in my sixth period art class and the three of us walk to class together when we leave the dining hall. Okay, more like Harlyn and Zade walk together and I sort of follow closely behind them.

Art class is located in Radcliffe Hall in this amazing space where all the walls are glass panels that allow natural light to flow into the room. The space is intimate with only five work stations set up throughout the room. We're greeted by a ruggedly handsome man who looks to be in his late twenties. He's got dark brown hair, light grey eyes and the shadow of a beard gracing his angular jaw. His clothes and hands are splattered with dried paint.

"Welcome," he greets us with a warm smile.

"What's up Professor Kipp," Harlyn says, her mouth splitting into a naughty smile.

"Harlyn," he says nodding in her direction.

I look from Harlyn to the Professor. It feels like these two have more than a teacher-student relationship going on. I'll have to ask Harlyn about it later.

Two more students enter the classroom and stand behind us. A short girl with fiery red hair and a splattering of freckles across her nose and a Latin boy with a mop of curly black hair framing a very handsome face.

"So, what's the setup this year, Professor?" Harlyn asks.

Professor Kipp claps his hands together and looks at us, his eyes dancing with excitement. "As you can see, class is much smaller this year. Only five of you. You each have your own station and I've placed you strategically based on your student profiles." He moves into the middle of the room. "Zade, you're back there in the far left corner. Harlyn, you're next to Zade. Melanie," he says pointing to the pretty redhead. "You're at the station in front of Harlyn, Andrew, you're at this station here," he says pointing to the workstation at the front of the room." He turns to me. "And you, Ms. Gamble, will be at the work station in front of Zade."

Great. I have to create art knowing that Zade Amherst is stationed behind me and potentially watching my every brush stroke. Talk about nerves. The guy already puts me on edge.

We all make our way to our designated stations. I marvel at all the supplies available to me. The highest quality paint brushes and canvases, all kinds of sculpting tools, modeling clay and so much more. It's an artist's dream.

"Today, I want you to simply create," Professor Kipp says. "No rules, no restrictions. Just create what you feel. We have coveralls for each of you over here," Professor Kipp says pointing to a wall where five white painter jumpsuits hang. "I'll be there in my studio if you need me," he says pointing to a room off to the side before disappearing into it.

Melanie and Andrew grab their coveralls, head to their stations and get to work. Zade grabs his and walks back to his station. I watch as he unbuttons his shirt revealing a wife beater that clings to a well-defined chest and flat stomach. My eyes travel across the expanse of his chest to a pair of sculpted arms covered in tattoos. He's just all kinds of bad boy goodness.

"Careful, Stray, you're drooling," Harlyn says and tosses me the last coverall.

Stains of scarlet darken my cheeks as I catch the coverall and slip it on over my uniform. I look back at Harlyn who's already got a large canvas out and has started to paint. I chance a look back at Zade and my gaze clashes with his blue-violet eyes. There's a heat to them as he looks at me, his eyes taking a lazy roam over my face, down my body and back up. His gaze is downright pornographic. I feel completely naked and totally vulnerable. I quickly turn around and face my own workstation. I have no idea how I'm going to get through a full year of this class with Zade Amherst working behind me.

By the time the bell rings indicating the end of sixth period, I'm in the beginning stages of a painting that I cannot quite figure out just yet but I like where it's going.

"Nice start, Stray," Harlyn says as she passes by me and heads out the door.

Melanie and Andrew leave out behind her leaving only Zade and I in the room. The scent of black licorice and cola swirls around me invading my scenes and without turning around I know that Zade is standing right behind me. I swallow the spit that's gathered on my tongue and turn around.

Why did I do that? His dark, dangerous beauty is overwhelming. And that blue-violet gaze of his is all consuming.

"How long you been painting?" Zade asks, his deep, smooth voice caressing me like a warm breeze.

"Since before I can remember," I manage to get out.

He moves in close, our bodies just a whisper away from touching. He leans in looking over my shoulder at my canvas behind me. "You've got some serious skills, Stray," he says.

"Thanks," I say. I should be annoyed that he keeps calling me Stray but it's hard to care about that when he's so damn mesmerizing. I inhale deeply taking in his intoxicating scent. *Gawd! He smells good.* I bite my lip to keep from moaning.

He pulls back but stays well within my personal space, his eyes penetrating me as if he wants to know every part of me. I feel like I should run. Get as far away from him as possible because deep down I know he's nothing but trouble and heartache waiting to happen but I can't move.

He leans in, his nose and mouth just inches from mine. His blue-violet eyes linger on my mouth and for a second I think he's going to kiss me.

"Later, Stray," he says then slowly backs away. His eyes twinkle with mischief.

I stand there like an idiot watching him leave. It's all I can do. I'm too shaken to move.

"Hey," Devya says as I walk out of art class.

"Hey," I say.

"I figured you'd have no idea how to get to the gymnasium so I figured I come by and walk you over."

"Thanks," I say, with an appreciative smile.

"How was art class?" She asks.

"It was kind of weird," I say, not sure of any other way to describe what I experienced in art class. Having Zade behind me while I worked. Feeling the heat of his gaze on me was a lot.

"Weird how?" Devya asks.

"I don't know. I mean the Professor is super cool and gives us the freedom to create what we want and the class has every art supply an artist can dream of. But it's a small class. Only five of us."

"So, what's weird about that?" Devya asks, her brow furrowing in confusion.

"It's not the class that's weird. It's more of who is in it."

"Are you talking about Zade?" She asks a knowing smile gracing her lips.

My stomach knots at the mention of his name. "There's just something about him, Devya. He's unnerving. And the way he looks at me, like...I don't know..."

"Like he's undressing you with his eyes?" She says finishing my sentence.

"Exactly!" I exclaim.

"That's Zade Amherst. Dark, brooding and sexy as fuck. Every girl here wants a piece of him," Devya says.

"Even you?" I ask.

She sighs. "Nah. The boy is hot but he's not really my type. I go for a more clean cut, boy next door look."

"So, what's his deal exactly? He doesn't say much and he's super hard to read."

"Zade Amherst is complicated and there's not enough time between here and the gymnasium to give you the full rundown but I'll come to your room tonight and give you the real scoop on everybody," she says wiggling her eyebrows.

"What's up, Devya?" A good-looking boy with dirty blonde hair, light blue eyes and a nice tan says as we pass through the courtyard on the way to the gymnasium.

"Hey Cord," Devya says, her mouth splitting into a flirty smile.

"Hit me up later so we can catch up," he says with a wink.

"I might," she says coyly and keeps walking.

"Ummm, who was that?" I ask.

"That was Cord Michelson. The sole heir to a twenty billion dollar fortune. Not to mention he's super smart and hot as fuck."

"Are you guys like a thing or something?" I ask.

"Hardly. We're just in the flirty phase. You know texting, following each other on IG and liking each other's posts."

"Well, he seems pretty into you if you ask me."

"I know, right." She says.

The gymnasium is located next to the auditorium. The front of the building is all glass windows and there's a marquee at the top of the building with the words, Home of the Bradford Eagles, on it.

"Here we are," Devya says gesturing towards the building.

"Thanks for walking me over," I say.

"It's no biggie. I mean I was assigned to show you around so it was kind of my job," she says with a shrug.

"Still I appreciate it," I say.

"Okay, so do you think you can find your dorm room or do I need to meet you here after class?"

"I think I can manage. Student housing is that way, right?" I ask pointing towards the set of buildings across the other side of the courtyard.

"You remembered. It takes some kids weeks to learn the layout of this place but yeah, just follow the path to the left from the auditorium and you'll run right into them."

"Okay," I say looking in the direction she's talking about.

"I better get to class," she says, starting to walk off. "I'll come by your room later. I'll bring dinner."

"Sounds good," I say as I watch her make her way back the way we came.

I've never been a big fan of physical education and I'm even more adverse to it now seeing how Bexley and Indigo are in my gym class. Just what I don't need.

They're on me as soon as I step out of the locker room in my school provided gym clothes of a pair of tiny, black shorts and a grey t-shirt with the words Bradford Academy printed on the front.

Bexley and Indigo are holding court in the middle of the gym surrounded by a group of girls hanging on their every word.

"Well, if it isn't the stray bitch," Bexley says and the girls around her all laugh.

I just roll my eyes and stand off to the side hoping that the gym teacher shows up soon.

Bexley saunters over to me, a look of sheer hate in her eyes. "Did you guys know that the mother of our little stray was the cause of her daddy dying?"

"What? That's not true," I say, shock and disbelief at the nerve of his girl.

"It is so. I heard my parents talking about you when they found out that Grandpa Gamble took you in. They couldn't believe he would do that seeing how he and his wife blamed your mother for their son's death. You're mother's a total murderer." She spits out the words contemptuously.

Immediately there's a deep pain in my chest as my heart constricts. How can she say such things about my mother knowing that she's dead? What kind of heartless bitch is she? Anger, raw and feral boils in my stomach. I clench my fists at my sides trying to keep myself together. "Don't ever talk about my mother," I say, my voice cold and lashing.

"Or what?" Bexley says stepping up to me. "What are you gonna do, Stray?"

"Mention my mother again and you'll find out."

"Your dead mother is a murderer," she sneers.

I'm blinded by tears and before I know it my hands are shoving into Bexley pushing her hard. She stumbles back a few feet then charges towards me.

"Oh, it's on," she says slapping me so hard my head spins and I stagger back.

I bump into Indigo who pushes me to the ground. I look up to see the entire class of girls surrounding me, closing in on me. *This is not going to end well for me.*

"Hold her down," Bexley says and four girls move forward each grabbing an arm and a leg.

I flail around trying to make it as hard as possible for them to maintain their hold.

Bexley stands over me, her legs straddling each side of my body. She bends down, her face just inches from mine. "You don't belong here, Stray. And I'm going to spend every waking moment torturing you until you get the picture."

"Fuck you," I spit and she slaps me hard across the face not once but twice. My cheek is stinging but I press my lips in a firm line and lift my chin defiantly. This bitch will not break me.

"Oh, she thinks she's tough," Bexley mocks me. She raises her hand to slap me again when the teacher walks in.

"What's going on here?" She asks, making her way over to us.

The girls holding my arms and legs immediately release me and stand up. The girls form a wall in front of me so the teacher can't see me.

"Hey, Miss Miller. We were just goofing around while we waited for you to show up," Bexley says, her voice syrupy sweet.

"Well I'm here now so spread out so we can stretch," she orders. The girls fan out leaving me lying on the floor and rubbing my stinging cheek.

"What's your name?" Miss Miller says walking over to me.

"Fallon Gamble."

"Ah, the new kid. You okay?" Miss Miller asks, studying me. From the way she's looking at me I can tell that she knows I'm not okay but I guess she's waiting to hear me say it.

I look over at Bexley who is scowling at me. I want to tell Miss Miller what she and the other girls did but Devya's words from this morning come back to me. *Try not to get on her bad side. Her family donated like half the buildings on this campus so she gets away with a lot here.*

"I'm fine. We were just goofing around," I lie.

Miss Miller sighs and pity flashes across her face for a brief moment. "Okay," she says then moves away from me.

"Indigo, lead everyone in stretching. And get real limber because we're playing dodgeball."

Great! I already know how this is going to go.

By the end of class, I'm winded, tired and there's pain shooting throughout every part of my body. We all know there's nothing friendly about dodgeball but try being the most hated person playing. I was the main target for every single person on the other team. Not to mention my own teammates shoving me about and leaving plenty of space around me making me an easy target. I got hit in the face with so many balls I'm nervous to even look at myself in the mirror.

"Fallon," Miss Miller calls as we're making our way into the locker room. "Come here please."

I make my way over to her, secretly thankful that I don't have to be in the locker room at the same time as Bexley and her band of minions.

"Yes," I say as I reach her.

"How are you doing? You took a little bit of a beating out there. Seems like all the girls were gunning for you." Sympathy plays at the corners of her eyes.

"Maybe a little," I say, sarcasm lacing my voice.

"It's tough being the new kid at Bradford. Especially coming in your junior year, not knowing anyone and coming from a different background than the rest of the kids here."

She's got that right!

"I could tell you it gets easier but it won't. These kids are rich and entitled. They're used to getting their way and honestly their parents pay for this school so there's not too much faculty can do to them. You're going to have to figure out how to hold your own around here. And based on what I saw today, you're tough. You'll figure it out."

"Thanks, Miss Miller. The kids here are definitely a different breed but you're right, I am tough. I can handle whatever they throw at me."

"Just be careful," she says.

The locker room is empty by the time I get there, thankfully. I quickly change, toss my soiled gym uniform in the laundry bin and head out. I practically run the entire way to the dorms. I'm not trying to get ambushed by Bexley and her minions.

Thank goodness student housing is set up pretty easily. There are four dorms; Barringer and Amherst which are the girl's dorms and Smith and Winkler which house the boys.

I rush into Barringer Hall, room key in hand. Even though I have yet to see my actual dorm room. I got my room assignment five days before school started and the key arrived by messenger two days after that. My room is on the fourth floor so I hurry to the elevators and press the up button. My nerves are on edge as I watch the numbers on the digital panel light up indicating which floor the elevator is on. All I want is to make it to my room without running into Bexley or any of the other girls.

I sigh in relief when the elevator doors open and no one is inside. I rush in, hit the button for the fourth floor and lean back against the wall as the elevator makes it ascent.

Finding my room is easy seeing how there's only four rooms on the entire floor. I'm in room 406 which is the last room at the end of the hall. I nearly die when I open the door and see my room for the first time. It's amazing. It looks like a luxury studio apartment. The floors are hardwood and glossy and the color scheme is soft violets and deep purples. There's a California king bed with an upholstered headboard that reaches almost to the ceiling that's clearly the centerpiece of the room. There's a half-wall at the foot of the bed separating it from the living area which is decked out with a loveseat, matching chair and a coffee table. There's a massive television sitting inside the half-wall and there's a cute little desk and chair setup in the far corner of the room. The entire backside of the room is made of glass and there's a pair of sliding glass doors leading out to a balcony. Thick curtains hang from the ceiling. Those will come in handy keeping the sunlight out in the mornings when I'm asleep. There's a kitchenette with a small stainless steel refrigerator, a two burner stovetop sitting beneath a floating microwave, a small sink, and a lovely set of stark white cabinets floating above the dark, marble countertop. There's two sets of cabinets and a set of drawers under the counter. It's a really cute little space. Very economical.

There's a massive wardrobe along the wall next to the bed and I rush over and open it. It's jammed packed with school uniforms and the new casual clothes grandfather had purchased for me. I run my hand across the expensive garments. I still cannot believe they're mine.

I close the wardrobe and make my way over to the private bathroom which is just off the entrance. Like the rest of the mini apartment, the bathroom, of course, is very high end with marble floors and countertops, golden faucets, large claw foot tub and freestanding shower. My house in Nebraska was nice but this place with its fancy furnishings and top of the line appliances and fixtures makes my old house look like a shack.

It's been a hell of a day. My brain is on sensory overload from my new surroundings and my limbs are sore from the not so friendly game of dodge ball. I eye the shower and my muscles contract as if begging me to get in. I turn the shower to hot, strip naked and stand underneath the square rain shower head and let the hot water wash away the day.

CHAPTER SEVEN

I just finish pulling on a pair of leggings and my favorite over-sized Jimi Hendrix graphic t-shirt when there's a knock on my door. I move cautiously towards it hoping it's not Bexley or one of the other girls coming to harass me. I lean forward looking through the peephole careful not to touch the door.

"Fallon, girl, open the door. It's me, Devya and I brought Chinese," she says holding a takeout bag up to the peephole.

I release the breath I didn't realize I was holding and open the door.

"Bout time. I thought you were in here sleeping or something," she says breezing past me.

I shut the door and follow her to the sitting area. "I had to make sure you weren't Bexley or any of her minions," I say plopping down on the sofa.

Devya, who's pulling containers out the bag, stops and looks at me. Her eyes go wide and her hand flies to her mouth. "Oh my god! Your face. Your cheeks all bruised like you've been hit or something."

"That's because I was," I say, rolling my eyes.

"Did Bexley do that?" she asked, her brow furrowed in worry.

"Yeah. Bexley and every girl in my gym class." I say shaking my head, still not believing what happened today.

"Damn, Fallon. What exactly happened?"

"Let's see. I showed up to class, Bexley talked shit to me and then proceeded to have four girls in class hold me down while she slapped me in the face repeatedly."

"Where was Miss Miller?" Devya asked.

I shrug. "They let me go as soon as she showed up."

"Did you tell her what happened?"

I shake my head. "What good would that do? You said it yourself, Bexley is the Queen Bee. She clearly runs this school."

"Yeah but one of these days someone's gonna put her in her place," Devya says, staring at the food in front of her.

"Maybe," I say. "She already turned every girl in gym class against me. We played dodge ball but it was more like hit Fallon with the ball. I just don't get it. She's so cruel. How is it that people can't see that?"

"Oh, we see it alright. It' just...you don't understand how things work in our world." Devya says.

"What does that even mean? We all live in the same world. We're all here on planet Earth," I say, sweeping my arms out wide.

"But do we though? Really?" Devya says, her face serious.

I'm at a loss so I just look at her waiting for her to elaborate.

"Fallon, this world that you've been thrust into recently, the world of the uber wealthy and elite, it's not like the rest of the world. Real world rules don't apply to us. I mean, there are normal wealthy families out there who think they have it all and think they're running the show. They ain't running shit. Our families own those families. Our families," she says pointing to me then herself, "the Gambles, the Nadars, the Barringers, the Amhersts, the Radcliffes, we run shit."

I feel like I'm in one of those horrible teen television shows where the kids are super rich assholes who act and live like adults.

"What do you know about your father's side of the family?"

"Not much," I shrug. "My grandfather told me a few things."

"Your father's family is very powerful, Fallon. The Gambles have way more money than the Barringers and I think that makes Bexley nervous. I think that's why she's coming at you so hard."

"Or it could be that she's just a bitch," I say, rolling my eyes.

"I'm sure that has a lot to do with it too," Devya laughs. "But seriously, you've gotta start to understand the circle you're in now. You need to learn who these people are so you know how to move within our group."

"What if I don't want to be in the group," I pout flopping back against the couch.

"Too late for that. Your grandfather made that decision for you when he enrolled you in Bradford Academy," Devya says her face turning serious.

"I don't understand," I say.

"Let me break it down for you," Devya says folding her legs underneath her bottom. "Bradford Academy is the Harvard and Yale of boarding schools. Your family has to not only be extremely wealthy but they have to have certain connections. There's a hierarchy within the elite and that same hierarchy applies here at Bradford. The kids at the top of the food chain come from the wealthiest families and are what we call pure bloods."

"Pure bloods?" I say with a frown.

"Yeah, it means that your family wealth goes back many generations so you're born into wealth. It's the only life you've ever known."

"Are you a pure blood?" I ask.

"Yep" she nods.

"But I'm not," I say.

"No, you're not but you're a Gamble and that trumps everything."

"Why?" I ask. This is some secret illuminati shit she's talking and it's blowing my mind right now.

"Because the Gambles not only have wealth, they also have political power. The Gambles ran the inner circle for years then they lost their heir when your father died. No heir, no power. So, for a long time the Gambles had to yield to the Barringers but then you came along and even though you're not a pure blood, you're the future of the Gamble dynasty so the rules were changed to accommodate your existence and not everybody's on board with that."

"And by everybody you mean Bexley," I say.

She nods. "Next to the Gambles, the Barringers are it. That family is worth sixty-six billion dollars and with the Gambles out of the way the Barringers took over the inner circle. And here at Bradford, there was no Gamble legacy so Bexley Barringer became the *It* pure blood around here."

"So, what about the others? How do they fit in?" I ask.

"So, here at Bradford the Barringers have been at the top of the hierarchy for a long time. At least since the last Gamble heir went here."

"My father," I say.

"Right, but that was a very long time ago. So, it's been the Barringers ruling this place. That family owns one of the largest fashion and retail chains in the country. After the Barringers you have Alisander's family, the Davenports, who make their money in oil. They're worth about forty billion. Then you have the Nadars," she says pointing to herself. "My grandfather is a billionaire industrialist and philanthropist. We're worth thirty-eight billion. Then there's Zade's family, the Amhersts, who own the largest energy infrastructure firm in the country. They're worth about thirty-six billion. Next you have Harlynn's family, the Radcliffes, who are cousins of the Barringers."

My eyebrows go up in shock. "Bexley and Harlyn are related?"

"Yeah, they're cousins but they're nothing alike. So anyway, the Radcliffes are worth like thirty-five billion, then there's the twins Indigo and Tatum James who are the offspring of Hollywood actor Quincy James and billionaire heiress, Leyla Motsepe James. Leyla's family is the real power in that union. The Motsepe's family made their fortune in gold, metal and platinum. They're worth like thirty billion. Then there's the Lucca's family, the Caldwells and Chloe's family, the Norths. The Caldwells and the North's are not as wealthy as the rest of us. Their net worth is in the high millions but they're legacies."

"Legacies?" I question, leaning forward.

"Yeah, Lucca's the son of legendary NFL running back, Darren Caldwell. He went to Bradford back in the day. Anyway, after daddy Caldwell retired from the NFL, he partnered with the

Amherst family in some lucrative deals putting the Caldwells in the inner circle. As for the North's, their worth about five hundred million but they're deep into politics so they have an in with the government which makes them very valuable."

"So, let me see if I got this right. The hierarchy here is Bexley Barringer, Alisander Davenport, You, Zade Amherst, Harlyn Radcliffe, the twins, Indigo and Tatum, then Lucca Caldwell and Chloe North."

"You got it except..."

"Except what?" I say, raising an eyebrow at her.

"Except now that you're here, technically you're at the top of the hierarchy," she says with sly grin.

"Me? Yeah, right?"

"I know you don't realize it yet, but you will eventually. Again, you just need to learn how things work."

"It's all so complicated. Why can't we just be teenagers?" I wine.

"We are teenagers. Our bank accounts are just bigger and normal teenager rules don't apply to us," Devya says with a smirk.

I shake my head. "I guess. I still don't know how I'm going to keep everything straight."

"Don't worry. I'll help you," Devya smiles.

"Thanks, Devya. You're really cool." I say with a smile. "Not at all like the rest of the assholes around here."

She smiles back at me but it doesn't seem to reach her eyes. "Thanks."

"I do have one more question," I say.

"Shoot."

"Ruby Stratton? What happened to her?"

Devya stiffens and drops her gaze which makes me all the more curious and nervous about what happened to the girl.

"Fallon, I really don't like talking about it so I'll tell you this. Ruby Stratton transferred to Bradford last year. The school tried this thing where they gave out a scholarship and Ruby won the scholarship. She was a really smart and very pretty girl. She was also very vocal and made a lot of noise about how Bexley treated everyone."

"I'm sure that went over well," I say, my sarcasm clearly evident.

"Yeah," Devya grimaces. "Bexley didn't like it at all. She made Ruby's life a living hell and I'm not talking about the standard name calling and occasional physical altercations. She literally drove the girl insane."

"What do you mean?" I ask. Surely, she's being hypothetical.
"I mean she drove her insane. Ruby's in a mental hospital," Devya says, her eyes softening in sadness.

"Wait! What? How did she drive her insane?" This is crazy and I'm in complete shock.

"I don't really want to go into all the details. Ruby was my friend and it's not something that I like to talk about. Besides, we should eat. The food is probably getting cold."

I want to press Devya for more information. The more I know about Bexley and what she's capable of, the better. But looking at Devya, she clearly doesn't want to talk about anymore so I drop it. "Okay, I'm pretty hungry anyway," I say, grabbing the container of garlic noodles.

We spend the rest of the evening snacking and gossiping. It's well after eleven when Devya finally heads back to her dorm.

I'm jolted out of a deep sleep by the blaring sounds of Billie Eilish's "You Should See Me In A Crown." It's five a.m. which is hella early but I have my first session with the school counselor at six-thirty. I hop out of bed and make my way to the bathroom. I gasp when I see my reflection in the mirror. My bedhead is bananas. My tawny curls are a frizzy mess around my head and the bruise on my cheek has turned from crimson to a deep purple. I close my eyes shutting out the horrific reflection of myself. I've never been in a fight my entire life. Not that you can call what happened to me yesterday a fight. I was basically jumped which I would have never thought would happen to me. I was very well liked back at my old school. I've got to be careful around here. Keep my guard up at all times.

I take a quick shower, washing and conditioning my hair. I put on a little foundation which covers up most of the bruising on my cheek. I add a light coat of mascara and some lip-gloss before putting on my uniform. I grab my backpack and head towards the administration building where the counselor's office is located.

It's still pretty early so campus is quiet. There are a few students studying in the courtyard but they pay me no mind as I move quickly past them. I reach the administration building and I'm greeted by a charming older woman sitting at the receptionist desk. The name plate on her desk says Joanna Darling.

"Good Morning, dear. How may I help you?" She says, her smile warm and inviting.

"Hi, I'm Fallon Gamble."

Her eyes light up at the mention of my last name. "Welcome, Miss Gamble. We're happy to have you here at Bradford Academy."

"Thank you. I have an appointment with Mr. Blackmore," I say.

She looks at her computer and punches a few keys then looks back at me. "Yes, he's in his office already. Take the elevator up to the second floor. He's in room 201."

"Thank you," I say and head to the elevators.

The door to room 201 is open and I peek my head in. The room is empty. "Good morning," I call as I move into the office.

"Ah, Miss Gamble," a voice says from behind me.

I spin around to see an older man, probably in his early fifties standing there. He's dressed casually in dark slacks and a yellow button down. His greying hair is a bit mussed around his head and he's wearing a pair of small, round, wire-rimmed glasses.

He extends his hand out to me. "I'm Doctor Elliot Blackmore. It's very good to meet you."

I take his hand. "Nice to meet you," I say.

"Have a seat, Fallon," he says pointing to the small leather sofa against the wall.

I sit down and watch as he closes the door then grabs a notebook and pen from his desk before sitting down in the overstuffed, leather chair across from the sofa.

"So, how are things?" he asks.

"Fine, I guess." It feels a bit weird being here talking to a stranger.

"And how are you adjusting to Bradford? I know it can be hard starting a new school."

He has no idea. My first day was hell but do I really want to tell him that? I don't want to set off any alarms. "It's been okay," I say. Not the truth but not really a lie.

"Have you made any friends yet?" He asks, jotting something on the notepad.

"I guess I made one." I wait for him to ask anther question but he sits there looking at me, waiting for me to say more.

"Her name is Devya Nadar. She was assigned to be my tour guide for the day and we sort of hit it off. She's really nice."

Mr. Blackmore nods and jots something on his notepad.

"What about the other kids? How are they treating you?"

Like shit! "Okay, I guess."

"Fallon, you know our sessions are completely confidential. Anything you share in here stays between you and me. So, feel free to be honest."

"How long have you worked here, Mr. Blackmore?" I ask.

"About five years," he says, resting his chin on his fist as he looks at me.

"Then you already know how the kids are around here. You don't need me to tell you."

He studies my face, eyeing the bruise on my cheek. "How'd you get that?"

"Gym class. We played dodgeball. I was a popular target," I say with a twisted smile.

He doesn't respond to that. Instead he jots something down in his notepad.

CHAPTER EIGHT

"A lot has changed recently in your life. You lost your mother not too long ago, moved across the country, and started a new school. How are you emotionally?"

My breath catches at the mention of my mother. Tears border my eyes and I bite down on my lip and stiffen my spine to keep them from spilling over. Losing my mom was the worst thing to ever happen to me. It's like someone punched me in the gut and left a gaping hole. There are no words to express how I feel about losing my mom.

"You don't have to talk about it now. We'll be meeting every week. Just talk about it when you're ready, okay."

I nod, still fighting to hold back the tears.

The rest of the week pretty much goes how the first day went. The magnificent three basically ignore me, Bexley and her clique of minions harass and torture me every chance they get and Devya spends a lot of time trying to be the buffer between me and everyone.

I'm happy when Friday finally rolls around. I can lock myself in my room all weekend and not have to deal with these wretched kids for a few days.

I was able to escape gym class without any major bruises. Miss Miller had us on the track running and I discovered that I'm much faster than the other girls so I was able to keep a good distance between myself and them. Miss Miller asked me to hang back after class saying she wanted to talk to me about joining the track team but I really just think she was trying to give the other girls time to change and clear out of the locker room so I wouldn't have to deal with them. I appreciate her for that.

Not ten minutes after I make it to my dorm room, there's a knock at my door. I look through the peephole to see Devya standing there with a big cheesy smile and Harlyn standing next to her looking as cool and nonchalant as ever.

I open the door. "Hey, what are you guys doing here?"

Devya's wearing a super cute rounded low neckline bodycon dress. The top is stark white and the skirt is a glittery silver. The dress fits her like a glove, hugging her in all the right places. She has on a really cool and expensive looking necklace and matching bangles, her dark hair is thick, shiny and flows in lose curls around her shoulders and her makeup is dark and sultry. She looks hot as hell.

She's got a large Gucci duffel back slung across her shoulder. She pushes past me and sets the bag on my bed. "It's Friday," she says looking at me as if I should know what that means.

"Yeah, it's Friday." Harlyn mimics as she walks into my room. She's carrying a signature Louis Vuitton makeup case that she sits on the coffee table.

Harlyn's outfit is nothing like Devya's. Her outfit is super edgy and very cool. She's wearing the tiniest black skirt with striped thigh highs and a pair of tall, black combat boots that stop just below her knees. Her top is this white, thin and flowy scrap of material layered beneath this bad ass black, leather jacket. Her short hair is tucked haphazardly underneath a black skully and her makeup is dramatic and flawless as hell. No wonder she called me plain.

Frowning, I close the door and turn to face the girls. "So, it's Friday. And that means…"

Devya rolls her eyes. "Alisander's party is tonight. Duh!"

"Oh, that," I say, not a hint of enthusiasm in my voice.

Harlyn chuckles and Devya frowns at her.

"Fallon, it's the first party of the year. It sets the tone for the rest of the year. I know Alisander said all are welcome but that's not true."

"Well technically he said all hot girls are welcome," Harlyn says plopping down on the sofa.

"Whatever," Devya says rolling her eyes. "The point is that the who's who of Bradford will be at the party and you're now a part of the who's who so you have to be there. Is this your wardrobe? She asks already opening the closet doors.

"Yeah," I nod.

"Harlyn," Devya calls and motions with her hand for her to come over.

Harlyn joins Devya at my wardrobe, the two flip through pants and tops and discuss options for me as if I'm not even there.

"See anything you like," I say, the words coming out a tad bitchy.

They don't seem to notice. "You're pretty well stocked with the latest fashions so that's a good thing. We've got a lot to work with." Devya says then turns to me. "Go shower so we can get this makeover started."

I frown at her in protest.

"Go," she says, shooing me with her hand.

Reluctantly I head towards the bathroom. I take a long time showering not giving one fuck that they're waiting for me in the other room. I don't really want to go to this party anyway.

I finish showering and make my way back to the living area in my towel to find several outfits laid out on the bed and Harlyn's set up a make-up station on my desk.

"I really love the color of your hair. It's so full and curly. It just needs a little taming and some shine. Go let Harlyn do your makeup then I'll do your hair. After that we can choose your outfit." Devya grins.

I can feel the excitement bouncing off of her. She's really enjoying this.

"Have a seat," Harlyn says gesturing to the chair in front of her.

I sit down and stare nervously up at her.

"Chill," she says with a chuckle. "I got you. Your face is gonna look beat to death when I'm done."

She grabs my chin and moves my face from side to side, studying my features. "Decent eyebrows. We'll shape them up a bit, maybe do a smoky eye and a bold lip." She grabs a pair of tweezers and gets to work shaping my eyebrows. She spends about thirty minutes on my makeup then calls Devya over to work on my hair which actually doesn't take that long.

"Time to pick out your outfit," Devya says.

"Okay, just give me a minute," I say, heading for the bathroom.

"Unh-unh," Devya says grabbing my arm and pulling me towards the bed. "You cannot see yourself until the entire look is complete."

"Fine," I sigh.

"We've narrowed it down to three options," Devya says waving her hand over the outfits laid out on my bed.

The first one is a super sexy, yellow patchwork, sequin bodycon deep V-neck mini dress. It's flashy and loud and will definitely draw a lot of attention. The second outfit is a pair of leather skinnies and a thin almost see-through grey crop top and the third outfit is a pair of fancy, pink booty shorts with a flowy black top, cropped leather jacket and fishnet stockings.

All three are super cute but I think I'd feel the most comfortable in pants so I choose outfit number two. "That one," I say pointing to the leather skinnies.

"Good choice," Harlyn says, her perfectly painted mouth tipping up in a smile.

Devya rolls her eyes. "That's because it's the one you picked out."

"Yeah, and the girl clearly has good taste." Harlyn bites back.

"Whatever," Devya says dismissing her. "Get dressed, Fallon," she says returning her attention to me.

I grab the outfit and move towards the bathroom.

"Where are you going, you dope?" Devya says.

"To the bathroom to get dressed," I say, looking at her like she's crazy.

"No, you can't see yourself until we're sure that everything is put together and looks right. Just get dressed right here. We're all girls. It's not that big of a deal," she says barely holding her patience in check.

"Fine," I say and take off my robe and quickly slip into the pants and top.

Devya comes over and messes with my hair before spinning me around so Harlyn can get a look at me.

"We do good work," Harlyn says, looking me up and down. Her eyes linger on my top which is pulled taunt across my breasts.

I shiver a little under her gaze and there's a light tickle in my belly. I don't know what to make of it so I ignore it and turn to Devya. "Can I go see myself now?" I ask.

"C'mon," she says and practically drags me to the bathroom.

I'm at a complete loss for words when I see myself in the mirror. I look like a freaking rock star. My hair is shiny and perfectly coifed, my make-up is dramatic and sultry and the outfit fits me perfectly. The leather skinnies show off the nice curve of my thighs and the halter top gives just the right glimpse of my flat tummy and hugs my breast just right so they look full and plump.

"Wow!" I say.

"I know, right," Devya squeals. "You look so fire, Fallon. The boys are gonna be shook when they see you."

"And the girls are gonna be pissed," Harlyn muses.

"We should head out. It's gonna take us about forty-five minutes to get to Alisander's house," Devya says.

"Not if I drive," Harlyn says with a smirk.

"Last time you drove, I nearly got whiplash," Devya whines.

"Then wear your seatbelt," Harlyn says.

"Fine. But it better not wrinkle my outfit," Devya says. She grabs her purse and cell phone off the counter and moves towards the door.

I grab the tiny purse with the silver chain strap that the girls laid out for me and drape it across my shoulder then grab my cell phone and follow Harlyn and Devya out the door.

The walk to Harlyn's car is pretty uneventful. Several kids are hanging out in the courtyard while others are dressed up and heading to their cars in the parking lot. I look around for the metallic purple Aston Martin but don't see it. I guess Alisander is already gone. Makes sense since the party's at his family's house. I don't see any of the pure bloods but there are a lot kids getting into fancy cars and speeding out of the parking lot.

I follow Harlyn and Devya to a black Porsche 911. It's a beauty. Very sleek and sporty. Harlyn gets in the driver's side and Devya climbs in the back of the passenger side.

"You can sit up front," I offer her. It only feels right that I sit in the back seeing how I'm the new girl here.

"No, I'm good. You sit up front," she says, smiling sweetly.

I slide into the buttery soft seat and remembering what Devya said about Harlyn almost giving her whiplash, I fasten my seatbelt.

I take in the interior of the car and I'm immediately in love. While the outside is flashy and athletic the inside is laid-back and cool. The interior is all black and outfitted for comfort and convenience with its sport steering wheel, touchscreen display, Apple CarPlay system and push start engine just to name a few of the amazing things about this car.

"She's a real beauty, isn't she?" Harlyn says starting the engine.

"She really is," I nod.

"Let's get this show on the road, ladies," Harlyn says, smashing on the gas.

The Porsche speeds forward and I'm slammed back against my seat from the force of it.

"That's why I'm sitting in the back," Devya chuckles.

Harlyn was right. With her driving, we get to Alisander's house in no time. She kept her foot pressed to the gas the entire time. I honestly don't think she hit the breaks even once.

After exiting the highway, Harlyn turns down a private road leading to a gated entrance on a secluded hilltop. She brings the car to a screeching halt in front of some large iron gates and rolls her window down. There's a small callbox sitting outside the gate. She presses the button.

"Speak," a male floats through the box. I can't be sure but I think it's Alisander.

"It's Harlyn. Open the gate you, dick."

"Fuck you, Harlyn," the boy says.

A few seconds later the gate opens and Harlyn speeds through. The driveway leading to the house is long. We pass by several acres of beautiful landscaped flora and large oak trees before the driveway curves and ends in a rounded circle surrounding a large fountain. The driveway is already packed with expensive cars. We get out and my jaw nearly drops to the floor. The house is spectacular. It's huge. More like a mansion really. The exterior is done in this beautiful ivory and cream masonry and there are large bay windows everywhere. A group of kids are hanging out in front of the house smoking weed.

"Hey Harlyn," a cute brunette with dark blue eyes and porcelain skin says.

"What's up, Skylar," Harlyn says walking up on the girl and pulling her tight against her body, her hands roaming the girl's backside before settling on her ass.

"Nothing. Just been waiting for you to call," the girl says her voice turning pouty.

"My bad, doll. I got busy but I'll find you later on tonight, okay," Harlyn says then kisses the girl on the mouth before releasing her and walking into the house. The girl stares after her completely dazed and utterly sprung.

An uneasy feeling bubbles in the pit of my stomach as I watch the flirty exchange. There's something about seeing Harlyn flirting and kissing someone that makes me feel...hell, I don't know what I'm feeling. I just know I don't particularly like seeing her kiss someone else.

"Ready to have some fun?" Devya says, looping her arm through mine as we walk into the house.

The interior of the house is just as spectacular as the outside with its limestone walls, humongous fireplace, floor to ceiling windows everywhere and shiny hardwood floors. And that's just the great room as you enter the house.

Rap music blares from a DJ booth set up on the second floor landing that overlooks the great room and green and blue laser lights flash all around the room. There are kids everywhere;

dancing, drinking and talking in small groups.

"Let's get drinks," Harlyn says and leads us through the great room and into the kitchen. That's where we run into Lucca making out with some girl. She's sitting on the counter and Lucca's standing between her thighs, his hand under her skirt as they make out.

"Really, Caldwell?" Devya says a disappointed look on her face.

Lucca turns around, a shit eating grin on his face. "Get lost," he tells the girl whose skirt he just had his hand up. Without protest she hops off the counter and leaves the kitchen.

"What's up Devya? You look hot as shit in that dress," he says, turning on the charm.

"I know," Devya says doing a little turn to show off the back of her ensemble.

"What's up Harlyn?" Lucca says before turning and locking his gaze on me. His brown eyes narrow and his head cocks to the side as he takes me in starting at my face then moving his gaze down my chest, over my belly, down my thighs and back up again. "Damn," he whispers. "Devya, is that your stray looking hot as fuck?"

Devya and Harlyn burst out laughing. Meanwhile, I'm standing there feeling completely vulnerable and slightly aroused from the way Lucca is looking at me which is nuts because he just called me a stray.

"She's hot, isn't she?" Devya says.

"Very," Lucca says and starts to move towards me. He's looking at me like I'm his next meal.

I start to move backwards as he closes in. I'm able to take about three steps when my back presses into the counter.

He straps me, bracing his arms on either side of me. "You clean up nicely, Stray," he says, his eyes on my mouth.

"Fallon. My name is, Fallon," I say, not able to help the breathy way the words come out.

He reaches a hand up and runs a finger along the column of my neck. My skin, where his fingers touch, tingles and burns. He moves in a little closer, his front brushing up against mine. Fire and heat sizzle around us. His mouth is just a breath from mine now and I just know he's going to kiss me. And I want him to. I mean, he hasn't been the most welcoming but he hasn't been that much of a dick either. And he's so damn hot.

"Oh, my gawd, Lucca! I've been looking everywhere for you," Tatum James says, stumbling into the kitchen.

Lucca whips around and moves to steady her, leaving me standing there breathless and overheated.

"Who is that?" Tatum asks trying to look over Lucca's shoulder. "Are you in here making out with some rando? Who is that back there?"

"That's nobody, girl. C'mon, let's go dance," Lucca says ushering Tatum out of the kitchen.

Devya rushes over to me. "Oh, my gawd! Lucca is so completely hot for you," she squeals.

"Seems to me like Lucca's hot for anything with two legs," I say trying to downplay what just happened.

"If you say so," Harlyn says handing me a red solo cup then handing one to Devya.

I take a look inside the cup. It's filled to the top with some dark brown liquid.

"Rum and coke," Harlyn says.

"I don't really drink," I say handing the cup back to her.

She doesn't take it. "Just nurse that one all night so you don't look like a square," she says then leaves the kitchen.

Devya and I follow Harlyn out into the great room which is now packed wall to wall with kids dancing.

"Let's set this motherfucker off," someone yells into a microphone and I look up to see Alisander perched on the second floor railing, legs dangling, and microphone in hand. The crowd below erupts and the DJ turns the music up louder and the kids start dancing harder.

"This is nuts," I yell over the music.

"I know right," Devya says and tips her cup to me for a toast.

I tap my cup against hers and take a sip of my drink and immediately frown. There's not much coke in the rum and coke that

Harlyn made.

"I'm gonna go dance. I'll see you guys later," Harlyn says and makes her way over to the brunette from earlier and the two start dancing.

So, far things have been pretty chill. I only ran into one of the girls and luckily, she was too drunk to recognize me. Good thing Lucca took her out of the kitchen before she did.

I look around the room trying to be nonchalant but secretly searching for Bexley. I need to keep my guard up because I know when she finds out I'm here it's going to lead to trouble.

"Hey Devya," Cord says, walking up to us.

"Hey, Cord," Devya smiles. "Do you know Fallon?"

Cord cuts his eyes at me then looks back at Devya. "She's the new girl, right?"

Devya nods. "Her grandfather is Wilson Gamble."

Cords eyebrows raise in surprise. "There's been a lot of talk about the new girl but nobody really uses her name."

"Let me guess. They refer to me as the stray, right?" I say.

"Yeah, they do," Cord says matter-of-factly.

I just sigh and take a sip of my drink. Just as I do, someone grabs me from behind and spins me around. My drink goes sloshing over my cup and spills onto the floor.

"Hey!" I yell.

"Don't worry about that. The help will get it later," Alisander says a cocky grin on his face and his hands resting on my waist. He smells like coconut and weed. Not a bad combination on him.

"What are you doing?" The music is so loud that I have to yell.

Alisander leans in, his mouth brushing my ear. "Lucca said you were here and that you looked hot as shit. He was right, Stray. You look good. Totally fuckable," he grins. It's infectious but not meant to be kind so I press my lips into a firm line to stop the smile threatening to grace them. I mean honestly, he just called me Stray *again.*

Dance with me," he says pulling me into the throng of people.

"Nah, I'm good. I don't want to spill my drink," I yell after him.

He ignores my protest, takes my drink from me and hands it to some kid I've never seen before then pulls me flush against his body. I grab his upper arms to steady myself and feel a slight tremble in his hard biceps beneath my fingers. He starts grinding his pelvis into mine and something tightens in my lower belly.

I know I shouldn't be enjoying this but the feel of his hard body against mine just feels so damn good. I wrap my arms around his neck and sway my hips in time with his. He presses his forehead to mine and our breaths mingle as we lock eyes.

"You really do look good tonight," he whispers, then brings his hand to cup the side of my face.

I watch in slow motion as he leans in and presses his lips against mine. Initially, I'm shocked that this is even happening. First of all, I'm kissing a boy I barely know and second, said boy hasn't really been all that nice to me. But when his lips seek mine ardently, I melt into him and allow his tongue to sweep the inside of my mouth.

"What the fuck!" Comes a high pitched scream from behind me.

Alisander breaks the kiss and steps back.

I turn to see Bexley standing there fuming. She's dressed in a killer baby blue bodysuit that hugs her in all the right places. Her glossy, blonde hair flows wavy around her face and shoulders and her make-up is flawless. She looks like she stepped straight out of a high fashion magazine.

"You bitch! You think just because you put on some new clothes and got your hair and make-up done that you can come up in here and do whatever you want?"

People stop dancing to watch us and the DJ lowers the music making it easier for people to hear.

"You know there's a saying in Texas. You can put lipstick on a pig but it's still a pig," she spits and tosses her cup of beer all over me.

"Oh shit!" Alisander says and bursts out laughing. All the kids around us join in and start laughing too.

My entire body starts to shake, my heart thunders in my chest and blood pounds in my ears as the sour stench of beer runs down my face. I look around the crowd of faces searching for Devya or Harlyn but don't see either of them. I look over at Bexley who's wrapped around Alisander as they both stand and laugh at me.

It's all becoming too much. I can feel the tears welling and I refuse to let them fall in front of these assholes. I push my way through the crowd and race down one of the dimly lit hallways.

I push open the door to the first room I come to only to stop cold at the sight of Zade. He's got some girl bent over the dresser and he's fucking her.

He looks over at me but he doesn't stop. His eyes just narrow and sparkle with some unreadable emotion.

I stand there covered in beer, mouth gaping in shock at what I'm seeing.

"You just gonna stand there and watch," he snaps in that raspy voice of his.

I turn and hightail it out of there. I don't stop until I'm outside the house. I find my way to Harlyn's Porsche and luckily the door is unlocked. I climb inside and curl up on the backseat. My body is hot with frustration and I feel like punching something or someone. Preferably Zade for being so damn hot and for fucking that girl right in front of me as if me being there didn't make any damn difference at all.

I don't know long I laid in the back of Harlyn's car but it had to have been quite some time. I sit up when driver's side door opens.

"Holy shit, Fallon. We've been looking everywhere for you," Harlyn says climbing into the car.

"Well you found me," I say, my voice thick with pain.

"Devya's still inside looking for you. We heard what Bexley did. Are you alright?"

"No, I'm not alright. Once again super bitch, Bexley, has totally humiliated me." I close my eyes in frustration. "Can you just go get Devya so we can leave," I say, really wanting to leave and go home and hide out.

"Sure. I'll be right back," she says, then heads back to the house.

A few minutes later she returns with Devya and the two get into the car.

"Jeezus, you stink," Devya says rolling down the window.

"She's covered in beer, genius," Harlyn snaps.

"Oh yeah." Devya turns in her seat to look back at me. "I'm sorry that Bexley did that to you. She gets territorial when it comes to Alisander."

"What are they like a couple or something?" I ask.

"Not really. I mean they both screw around with other people all the time but their families have connections through business dealings and whatnot and their parents have it in their heads that those two will end up together."

"True but I think it's more than just the fact that Alisander has the hots for you. I think that my cousin is a little threatened by you," Harlyn says, looking at me through the rearview mirror.

"Why? Because my family has more money than hers?"

"That and because you're a fucking hottie. And I know that the guys treat you like shit but they're not blind. You looked good tonight and Lucca and Alisander noticed."

I wonder if Zade noticed. The only time I saw him tonight was when I walked in on him fucking that girl which even now makes me sick to my stomach. *Seriously, Fallon! What is wrong with you? You were just assaulted and embarrassed by these kids and you're worried if Zade Amherst noticed you. And what do you care if Zade noticed your makeover anyway? You literally just walked in on him having sex with someone.*

"I really don't care that they noticed. I don't want anything to do with either of them," I say, knowing the words are a lie as soon as they leave my mouth.

CHAPTER NINE

It's more of the same as the weeks go by. Being at Bradford is like being a hamster trapped on a wheel. No matter where I go, I'm constantly running into one of the pure bloods. They're everywhere and since the party, Bexley and her minions have amped up their harassment.

Indigo and Tatum ruined my lab experiment in chemistry class by pouring some unknown substance in my beaker and causing it to overflow and make a huge mess at my work station. We played softball in gym and Bexley made sure to chuck the ball at me every chance she got. I was able to duck out of the way most of the time but I have a few purple and black bruises on my back and thighs from the hits I wasn't able to avoid. It seems like everyone's fine watching me be tortured on a daily basis. Everyone but Zade, who's barely looked at me since the party. And when he does it's with a scowl.

The only time I can really relax and let my guard down is when I'm hanging out with Devya and Harlyn in my room or theirs. Tonight, we're hanging out in Devya's room at Amherst Hall. Her room is just about the same size as mine and it's beautifully decorated. She's got a huge Maison canopy bed with gorgeous gold, blue and white linens. Her sitting area is fashioned in the same color scheme and her wardrobe is twice as big as mine and is overflowing with clothes and shoes.

"Damn, Devya, you're a freaking hoarder," Harlyn says with a laugh.

"I'm not a hoarder. I just have a lot of things," Devya says.

"Sure," Harlyn and I say in unison then burst out laughing.

"Whatever," Devya says laying across her bed. "Hey, Fallon, how are things in gym class? Have Bexley and the girls backed off any?"

"Hell no! Bexley takes every opportunity to torture me in that class. You should see the bruises I'm sporting on my thighs from the day we played softball," I say.

"That sucks," Harlyn says shaking her head. "My cousin's such a little bitch."

"Yeah, what's her deal anyway, Harlyn? You two are nothing alike." I say, hoping to get some insight on Bexley and what makes her such a super bitch.

"The life of the entitled is all I can say. Bex is my Aunt and Uncle's pride and joy. They've always coddled her and given her everything she's ever wanted. She's been the top of the food chain around here since freshman year with like zero challengers and then you come along. The Gamble heir. Your family has more money than any of ours. Bexley hates that."

"I'm not here to take her crown. She can keep it," I scowl.

"It's not about you taking it. It's already yours and she knows it," Harlyn says then looks at Devya.

"Harlyn's right. It's like I told you before, the Gambles are at the tip top of the elite food chain. Your grandfather runs shit again and you're his heir. That means that you're also at the top of the food chain even if you don't really understand what that means yet."

"This whole hierarchy, pure blood, top of the food chain stuff is bullshit. I didn't ask for any of this. I literally just lost my mother less than two months ago and I now I have to put up with shit from Bexley Barringer. I wish everything could just go back to the way it was," I finish on a sad note.

Devya comes and sits next to me and puts her arm around my shoulder. "I'm really sorry about your mom. And I'm sorry Bexley is making your life here at Bradford so shitty. You're a nice person. You really don't deserve what she's doing."

"But at the same time, you have to understand where she's coming from and how this new world you've entered works.

Things work differently in this circle. No one's going to reprim-
and Bexley for her bad behavior. You're gonna have to figure out
how to assert your position and take her down, Fallon," Harlyn
adds, her face serious.

"That's easier said than done. I'm just not used to kids behav-
ing this way. She would have been expelled at my old school."
I say. It's clear that no one is going to help me with this Bexley situation. I'm just going to have to figure it out on my own.
"Enough talk about Bexley and the illuminati. Let's talk about
something else."

"Illuminati?" Devya and Harlyn say in unison and burst out
laughing.

I grab two pillows and throw one at Devya and the other at
Harlyn. Devya ducks. Harlyn catches her and tosses a smirk my
way.

"Fine, changing the subject," Devya says, pursing her lips. "The
Annual Dare Party is coming up."

"Dare Party?" I look from Devya to Harlyn.

"Yeah, it's a tradition here at Bradford. Every year there's a
party that only the pure bloods are invited to. We're all assigned
a task that has to be completed before sun up. Anyone who fails
to complete their task gets fined a hundred stacks and shunned
by the pure bloods the rest of the year," Harlyn explains.

"Are you serious?" I ask completely shocked. What is this
place? And who are these people?

"As a heart attack," Harlyn replies.

"Okay but what if you don't have a hundred grand to pay up?' I
ask.

Devya and Harlyn look at me like I've sprouted another head.

"What do you mean? It's a hundred grand. That's chump
change," Harlyn says, with a shrug.

"Well I don't have that kind of money," I say.

"Didn't your grandfather set up an account for you?" Devya
asks.

"I don't know. I mean he gave me a black card to use in case I
need anything." I say.

"I'm sure the limit on your black card is high enough to cover it. But it won't come to that because you're gonna complete whatever task you're assigned." Devya says with enough confidence for the both of us.

I haven't spoken to my grandfather since he dropped me off at Bradford and I haven't used the black card once. I have no idea what the credit limit is. This Dare Party sounds crazy anyway. Not to mention, Bexley will be there and I really don't want another incident of her drenching me in alcohol. I think I should sit this one out.

"I don't think I'll be attending the Dare Party," I announce.

"Yes, will you. You're one of us now, Fallon," Devya says.

"Am I though? I'm not a pure blood like you guys."

"I know but like we've been saying, your family's at the top of the food chain. Your grandfather runs the show. He adjusted the rules for you so you're in," Devya says.

"It doesn't matter what you say, Fallon, your attendance at the party is mandatory," Harlyn adds. "Besides it'll be a chance for you to start to claim your territory. These tasks we have to complete aren't for the faint of heart and if you complete yours you'll win some respect."

I always figured that being a human being allotted me some general respect and decency but apparently not in these circles. I'm clearly going to have to nail whatever task I get at the party to gain some respect around here.

My sessions with Mr. Blackmore have pretty much consisted of him asking me how things are going and me giving him very basic and often vague answers. He clearly knows I'm having a hard time adjusting to Bradford but isn't saying anything. I think he's waiting for me to tell him what's going on which isn't going to happen. It's not like he can help me deal with Bexley or any of the other pure bloods anyway.

I sit on the couch in his office staring quietly at my shoes while he sits across from me, staring at me, waiting for me to talk.

After a good five minutes of silence he finally speaks. "So, Fallon, I know you like art. How's your art class going?"

"It's fine," I reply.

"And what about extracurricular activities? Anything you're interested in? Sports? Cheerleading? I was looking at your grades and you're doing extremely well in math. Ever thought about tutoring?"

I shake my head.

"Extracurricular activities look good on transcripts. Bradford has a pretty good volleyball team," he adds.

Volleyball? I don't think so. That's just setting myself up to be pummeled by flying volleyballs. No thanks! "I'm not really into sports," I say.

"What about tutoring? I know we need a few more tutors in our program. Especially for math."

I suppose not much can go wrong with tutoring. It's pretty low-key seeing how it's one on one and most people don't ever want to admit to needing help so they keep it on the low. "Okay, I'll try the tutoring thing," I say, giving in figuring he would just keep hounding me about it otherwise.

"Great!" Mr. Blackmore says and jots something down on his notepad.

I leave his office and head straight to chemistry class. I take a moment to mentally prepare myself before entering the classroom.

Tatum spots me as soon as I come in. "Do you guys smell something?" She says holding her nose.

Chloe squeezes her nose. "Ugh! All of a sudden it smells like stray bitch in here."

Indigo, who's practically sitting in Zade's lap looks up and hits me with her best bitch face. "Has no one put that stray down yet? Jeez!"

I ignore all three of them and take my seat. I eye Zade on the way. He's just sitting there in that quiet, bored and brooding way that he does. I notice his hand resting on Indigos thigh and my stomach knots. What is going on with those two? Indigo's all over him every time they're in the same room and he doesn't seem to mind. At the same time, he was just having sex with some girl at the party at Alisander's house. It's maddening. Zade Amherst is maddening.

At the end of sixth period Professor Kipp hands me a note. It seems I've been assigned to tutor someone. Mr. Blackmore didn't waste any time getting that set up.

My tutoring sessions take place during seventh period which means I get a pass out of gym class. I wasn't all that thrilled about this tutoring thing but if it means that I don't have to go to gym class and deal with Bexley, I'm all for it.

The note says that I'm to meet the student that I'm assigned to tutor in the faculty library located in the main administration building which I find very strange. Why on earth are we meeting in the faculty library? I've never tutored anyone before but I had a few friends back in Nebraska who did and they always met someplace public. Then again Bradford is nothing like my old school. In fact, I bet Bradford is not like any other school out there.

I find my way to the faculty library with no issue. It's in the main administration building on the first floor. There's a modest sign on the door that says Faculty Library with the words No Students Allowed underneath. I ignore the sign and open the door seeing how the note I'm holding says this is where I should be.

The room is spacious and neatly decorated with several dark wood tables and chairs, lovely paintings grace the walls and there are floor to ceiling bookshelves throughout the entire space. The room is quiet and I have yet to run into anyone as I move through the space.

"Boo!" Someone says from behind me.

"Jeezus!" I yelp as I turn around to find Lucca Caldwell standing there, a humorous grin on his face. "You scared the crap out of me."

"You need to be more alert, Stray," he says cocking his head to the side as he stares down at me.

"Or maybe you shouldn't sneak up on people," I retort. "What are you doing in here anyway?"

"I'm here to be tutored in math, duh. Isn't that why you're here? To tutor me," he says, looking at me like I'm dumb.

"Oh, I didn't know you're the one I'm tutoring," I mumble.

"Well I am so let's get started. I have practice in an hour," Lucca says and makes his way to one of the tables all the way in the back of the room.

I follow him and try not to stare at how good he looks from behind. His khaki's and button down do nothing to downplay his muscular physique. And that walk of his. All swagger and sex. I can't stop the blood pumping in my ears or the pounding of my heart.

Lucca sits down and I take the seat directly across from him.

"So, what do you want to cover?" I ask.

"Before we get started let's get a few things straight," he says.

"Okay," I say, leaning back and folding my arms across my chest.

"First of all, this tutoring thing needs to stay between you and I so don't go telling anybody," he says, his voice hard.

"I wasn't planning on it," I say.

"Good. I don't need folks giving me shit about being tutored by the Stray."

"Hold up," I say, folding my arms across my chest. "If I'm going to tutor you and keep it a secret you're going to have to call me by my name."

He narrows his eyes at me. "Fine. But you have to do something for me."

"I'm already doing something for you," I say pointing to the math book on the table.

He wets his lips and those brown eyes darken as they search my face. "Something else," he says.

Is it me or did his voice just drop an octave? I shift nervously in my seat as his gaze slides to my mouth and lingers for a few seconds before moving back up to meet my eyes.

"Wear your hair down when you meet me for tutoring," he says.

My hand automatically goes to my hair which is pulled into a messy bun on the top of my head. "Why?" I ask.

"Because you look hot with your hair down," he says as if it's obvious.

My body instantly heats. Is Lucca Caldwell coming on to me? Again? I haven't forgotten how he trapped me between him and the counter and almost kissed me at Alisander's party. The way he looked at me. The way he leaned into me. I was completely enamored.

I reach up and undo the bun letting my tawny tendrils fall around my face and shoulders.

Lucca's brown eyes seem to darken and smolder as he stares at me. He gets up and moves into the seat next to me and grabs a few tendrils of my hair. "You look like an angel," he whispers.

My stomach somersaults. Pretty ass Lucca Caldwell just compared me to an angel. And the way he's looking at me, like I'm the prettiest thing he's ever seen has me breathing heavy. He's so close to me. If I move just a few inches our lips will touch and the way I'm feeling right now, being in this close, quiet space with him, I so want to kiss him. I know he hasn't been the nicest to me but he also hasn't been the worst. Not that that's any justification. It's just that he's so damn gorgeous and for whatever reason there's this attraction between us. One that I know I should ignore. Will ignore. So instead of closing the distance between us and kissing him, I lean back. "I did my part. I let my hair down. Your turn," I whisper.

Lucca's mouth splits into a delicious smile as he lets the few tendrils of my hair he was fingering fall back to my shoulder. "Fine...Fallon. Let's get this tutoring thing started," he says leaning back in his chair.

We're not in the same math class but we're both taking pre-calculus so the work is the same. He's having some trouble with polynomial and rational functions which I break down for him. By the end of the hour he's got it down.

"You a pretty good tutor, Fallon. You broke that shit down way better than Professor Wong did," he says gathering his book and notepad.

"Thanks, I say, getting my own belongings together.

"So, I'll see you back here tomorrow, right?" He asks moving towards the door.

I follow behind him. "Yep."

He stops and turns to face me when he gets to the door. He leans against it, his thumb and finger playing gently at his bottom lip as he studies me.

My nerves spike and my belly tingles as I lock eyes with him. Suddenly I feel very hot. It's like someone cranked up the heat. "What are you doing?" I breathe out as I reach him.

He doesn't say anything. He just reaches his arm out, wraps it around my waist and pulls me to him. My breasts brush against his hard chest and my breathing immediately hallows out.

His eyes search my face. "I been wanting to kiss you since the party."

A wave of excitement washes through me at his words. I wanted him to kiss me at the party and I want him to kiss me now.

"I guess this is your second chance to make that happen," I say, then run my tongue across my lips wetting them.

Lucca doesn't waste a second. He quickly dips his head and captures my mouth pushing his tongue between my lips. I groan and lean into him and he tightens his hold on my waist.

Good lord, he tastes good. My body melts all the way into him and I wrap my arms around his neck, caressing the soft skin at the base. My heart is pounding and my pulse is racing as he swirls his tongue around mine sucking and tasting. His hands roam my back then travel down to my ass and back up again and I can't help the moan that escapes my mouth. I'm completely lost in his kiss.

Who knows how long we would have stayed there, in the faculty library, pressed against the door kissing if Lucca's phone hadn't started vibrating.

"Hold up," he says breaking the kiss.

We're both panting, eyes glazed and lips swollen. His arm is still wrapped around my waist when he reaches into his pocket and pulls out his phone.

"Shit! Its coach. I gotta go."

"Okay," I say and go to step back but he holds me in place.

He runs his thumb over my lips then leans down and presses his mouth softly to mine. "Don't forget our agreement, Fallon," he murmurs against my mouth.

I nod. It's all I can do. I'm too worked up to formulate words right now.

CHAPTER TEN

It's late, well after 11 p.m. when there's a knock on my door. Always cautious, I tip-toe to the door and peer through the peephole but don't see anyone. Something hits my foot and I look down to see an envelope under the door. I grab it and examine it closely, weighing it in my hand and shaking it trying to make out if there's something dangerous inside. It's crazy having to do this but I wouldn't put it past these jerks to send me an envelope full of itching powder, poison ivy or anything else that would make my life miserable.

I don't hear anything odd moving around in the envelope so whatever it is can't be that dangerous. I turn the envelope over to find my first and last name scrawled in cursive on the back and on the front, is a wax seal with the letters PB stamped into it. I have no idea what it is or who it's from but it has my name on it which peaks my curiosity so I break the seal open. Inside is a beautifully crafted invitation on rose gold paper dripping with glitter.

You are cordially invited to attend
The Annual Dare Party
Saturday, the twelfth of October at 7pm
A car service will arrive a 6:30pm to take you to the location of the party
This is a private event, invitation only.

I re-read the words on the invitation a few times. The Dare Party. This is what Devya and Harlyn were talking about. Even with all of Devya's talk about me being one of them I still can't believe I'm actually invited to this exclusive event. It's kind of exciting until I realize this means that I'll be at some private function at an unknown location with a bunch of spoiled, rich kids who hate my guts.

I think about calling Devya to talk about the invitation but it's late so instead I sit the invitation on the table and climb in bed to get some sleep. I'll talk to her about it tomorrow.

"Did you get your invite?" Devya says as she rushes up to me after chemistry class, excitement vibrating from every cell in her body.

I pull the envelope from my bag. "You mean this?"

"Yes, that," Devya says snatching the envelope and shoving it back in my bag. "You can't just go waving that about, Fallon. The Dare Party is extremely exclusive. Majority of the kids that go here have no idea it even exits."

"My bad," I frown.

Devya loops her arm through mine. "It's cool. You're new to all this."

"It's not cool," Indigo spits as she passes us on her way out of chemistry class with Tatum and Chloe in tow. Zade, who she's usually clinging to is not with them. He must still be in class.

"Indigo, she didn't know," Devya comes to my defense.

"I'm not talking about her waving the invitation around for everyone to see," Indigo says with a scowl. "It's not cool that this stray is even invited to the party. She's not a pure blood."

"Well, you don't make the rules, Indigo so you're just gonna have to deal with it," Devya finishes with a smug smile.

"Deal with what?" Zade asks stepping into the hall and standing between me and Indigo.

His licorice and cola scent wraps around me like a warm blanket. I have to stop myself from inhaling deeply and filling my nostrils with the very essence of him.

"The fact that Fallon got an invite to the Dare Party," Devya says, that smug smile of hers reappearing.

Zade narrows his blue-violet gaze at me, penetrating my soul and I shiver.

I swear every time he looks at me it's like my body goes up in flames. It's crazy because most of the time he looks at me with such disdain that I should probably be running in the opposite direction. Instead I want nothing more than to get lost in that blue-violet gaze, wrapped up in those big, strong arms, and drunk in that delicious scent of his.

"If I were you, I'd opt out," he says then throws his arm around Indigo's shoulders but his eyes are still fixed on me.

It's like he's taunting me. Standing there with his arm wrapped around her but his eyes on me. I really don't understand him at all. If he's trying to make me jealous, it's working. But then again, Zade Amherst doesn't seem like he cares enough to put on a charade just to make me jealous.

"You know she can't do that, Zade. She got an invite. If she doesn't show and complete her task things will get even worse for her than they already are," Devya says.

"Whatever," Zade says, in that I really don't give a fuck way of his. He tightens his grip on Indigo and leads her away. Tatum and Chloe follow close behind.

"What is his deal?" I say, letting out a frustrated sigh.

"What do you mean?" Devya asks.

"What do I mean? Devya, are you blind? Don't you see how he acts?" I shriek.

She cocks her head at me. "How does he act, Fallon?"

"You know...he's just...he's just so..." I can't even find the right words to express my frustration with Zade. "He's always lurking around all quiet and brooding. And what's up with him and Indigo? Are they like a thing? She stays hanging all over him."

"Fallon, do you have a thing for Zade Amherst?" Devya asks, her face masked in feigned innocence.

"What? No!" I sputter.

"Are you sure? You seem really pressed right now."

"You know what, forget it," I say and start walking to French class.

Devya catches up and falls in step with me. "Don't get mad. I'm just teasing."

I roll my eyes at her.

"Look, Zade Amherst is hot as hell. He has that whole quiet, dark, brooding thing down to a tee. Not to mention, he's wealthy as shit and he's a badass artist. Majority of the girls at Bradford are in love with him. But the guy's elusive. As long as I've known him he's never actually had a girlfriend in the traditional sense of the word. Now don't get me wrong. He bags many bitches and I mean a lot of them. And they all know about each other and they don't care. They're all just hoping that they'll be the one that he chooses in the end."

"That's nuts," I say.

"I know, but that's Zade Amherst. And as for Indigo, those two have been doing whatever it is they do for a few years now. I think their connection has something to do with their family's investments. The thing about being wealthy is that the families are always trying to partner up with other wealthy families to increase their wealth and strengthen their family name. I do know that if Indigo ends up with Zade it would be the merger of a lifetime. Combine all the money and clout of those two families and the inner circle will be turned on its head. They would rule the inner circle."

"Would he really be with her just to position his family in a place of power?" I ask, disbelief drawing the space between my eyes together.

"Fallon, in our world, people do crazy things for the survival, family name and fortune. You'll learn that eventually."

"Let's go losers. I made an appointment at this little boutique in Austin for us to pick out banging ass outfits for the Dare Party." Harlyn says. She's lounging on my sofa, arms behind her head, her studded leather ankle boots, that I know cost a small fortune, are kicked up on the coffee table.

"Alright," Devya calls from the bathroom. "Let me just finish putting on my makeup."

It's Saturday and we're just under a week away from the Dare Party. Harlyn and Devya talked me into going with them to Austin to find a dress.

"You look hot," Harlyn says turning her hazel gaze on me.

I look down at myself. I'm wearing a pair of distressed, black skinny jeans, an army fatigue crop top, and a pair of maroon Jordan's. I straightened my hair and it hangs, thick and glossy down my back. I'm not half the make-up guru Harlyn is but I did apply a light coat of foundation to smooth out my skin, some mascara and eyeliner to make my eyes pop and some super shiny lip gloss to give my lips that wet look.

"Thanks. I did what I could," I say with a proud smile.

She gets up and walks over to me, her eyes low and a dangerously flirty smile on her lips. She runs her thumb along the outer rim of my bottom lip. "Just cleaning up your gloss a little bit," she says her voice low and throaty.

The spot where she touched tingles and my body warms from the contact. She's standing extremely close and I don't mind it at all. She smells like apricots which is unexpected but nice. It's weird the reaction I have to Harlyn. I've never been into girls but then I've never met a girl like Harlyn Radcliffe.

"Are you flirting with me?" I ask.

She moves in a little closer, her body just barely brushing mine. "Yep."

"Just checking," I say and bite my lip. My eyes fall to her mouth which is really quite pretty. Her lips are full and billowy and look soft as hell. *Is it weird that I want her to kiss me?*

"You guys ready?" Devya asks coming out of the bathroom. She stops short and stares us, her eyes gape open wide. "What's going on?"

Harlyn steps back. "Just over here flirting with Fallon while we wait for you," she says as if it's no big deal.

Me, on the other hand, I'm hot with embarrassment. I have no idea what's come over me. I'm like a cat in heat with these Bradford kids. Lucca, Alisander, Zade and now Harlyn. What is life right now?

"Oh, well I'm ready if you guys are," Devya says grabbing her purse, completely unbothered.

Harlyn drives us to Austin in her Porsche doing well over a hundred miles an hour. She brings the car to a screeching halt in front of this cute little upscale boutique.

"We have the place to ourselves for the next two hours," she announces as she climbs out of the car.

"What does that mean?" I ask.

"It means I rented the place out for the next two hours so that you, me and Devya will be the only customers in the store," she says looking at me like I'm clueless, which I am.

"Where I come from you don't just close down stores for your own personal shopping experience," I say.

"Well it's a good thing you left that place behind," Harlyn says then makes her way to the entrance of the boutique.

"This is gonna be so fun," Devya says grabbing my arm and pulling me towards the entrance.

"Harlyn Radcliffe," a tall, blonde with electric blue eyes set in a soft, round face says as we walk in.

"Hey, Ramona," Harlyn says kissing the young woman on both cheeks. "These are my girls, Devya and Fallon," she says motioning to us.

"Hello," I wave.

Devya just smiles.

"Hello ladies," Ramona says. "We're extremely excited to have you here today. We've pulled a bunch of selections for you. Follow me."

Ramona makes her way to the back of the store and we follow. She leads us to a large room with a fancy white sofa strategically placed in front of two racks of clothes. There's a small table off to the side with champagne, fresh fruit and cheese on it.

Two young women stand by the racks of clothing with smiles

plastered on their overly done lips.

"This is Katie and Steph. They'll be your personal shoppers today. Anything you want, they'll take care of it." She motions to the table of drinks and food. "We've got some champagne and light bites over there in case you get thirsty or want a snack. Have fun, ladies," Ramona says then disappears out of the room.

Devya heads straight for the rack of clothes while Harlyn makes a beeline for the table and pours three glasses of champagne. She hands one to me and Devya then takes her glass over to the sofa and sits down.

"There are so many great options," Devya muses. She holds up a geometric, sequined sheath dress. "Oh my gawd! This would look amazing on you, Fallon. "It's Balmain. You have to try it on."

I have to admit the dress is really cute. The top is a bit racy with its deep v-neckline that goes all the way down to the waist line. I look at Harlyn.

"I think Devya's on to something. You should try it on," she says.

"I'll take that to one of the fitting rooms for you," Katie says. "Is there any other options you'd like me to pull for you?"

"No, I think I'll just try that one for now," I reply.

"Very good. Follow me please," she says and leads me a short way down the hall to a dressing room. She hangs the dress on one of the hooks then. "I won't be far. Just holler if you need me."

"Thank you," I say then step into the dressing room.

I slip into the dress and I'm floored with how good it looks on me. I rush out of the fitting room to show the girls.

"Damn, Stray! You look so fucking fire in that dress," Harlyn says.

Devya whips around. "Holy shit, Fallon. You have to get that dress. It's perfect."

"Really? This is the only thing I've tried on so far. You don't think I need to try on a few more?"

"No way," Devya says. "That's your dress."

"You sure?" I question even though I know the dress looks

good. My level of confidence around these kids has taken a hit and I need the extra reassurance.

"We're sure," they say in unison.

"Okay," I smile. "I'll take this," I say to Katie.

"Very good. Just leave it in the fitting room and I'll put it up front for you," Katie says.

I quickly change and join Harlyn on the couch. "Why aren't you picking anything out?" I ask as we watch Devya run Steph crazy. She has the poor girl loaded down with dresses and running back and forth to the fitting room.

"I already have my outfit for the party," she says taking a sip of champagne.

"Then why'd you plan this trip?" I ask.

"I figured a little time away from Bradford might be good for you. You know, get away from all the pure blood crap and my anus of a cousin, Bexley."

I can't help but smile. Harlyn really is a gem. The more time we spend together the more I like her. "Thank you. This was very thoughtful of you."

She just shrugs and keeps sipping her champagne.

Two hours and three empty bottles of champagne later, we are finally heading out. Me with my sequined Balmain which cost a small fortune and Devya with a beautiful Carolina Herrera floral off the shoulder cape silk mini-dress.

"You had a lot of champagne," I say to Harlyn when we get to the car. "Are you good to drive?"

She tosses me her keys. "Here, you drive," she says. "You barely drank one glass."

I nearly drop the garment bag I'm holding trying to catch the keys. "Ummm...are you sure? I don't have my license yet."

"But you do know how to drive, right?" She asks her eyebrow lifting in question.

"Yeah."

"Okay, then. Unlock the doors and let's go," she says.

I hit the unlock button on her key fob and she gets into the passenger seat. Devya climbs into the back.

I slide into the driver's seat and the minute I push the button to the start the car I can feel the power of the engine and all I want to do is press my foot to the gas and smash out. I see why Harlyn drives so fast. You can't help it with a car like this. I do my best to be responsible and go the speed limit but Harlyn's not having any of that.

"Go ahead and open her up. You know you want to," she says a mischievous sparkle in her eyes.

She's right. I bite my lip and go for it. I do a hundred and ten easily all the way back to Bradford.

CHAPTER ELEVEN

October twelfth rolls around quickly and before I know it I'm at Devya's place getting ready for the Dare Party. Devya hired a celebrity hair and makeup artist for the occasion. I know I have a healthy disdain for these kids and how they use their wealth as a weapon but sometimes it comes in handy.

"So, what can I expect tonight?" I ask Devya as the makeup artist finishes working on my eyes.

"I can't really get into all the details but there will be a formal sit down dinner and a ceremony of sorts. After all that's done the real festivities start."

"Well that's not telling me much but okay." I say with a pout.

"Fallon, we don't really discuss this stuff in mixed company," she nods her head towards the stylist.

"Oh," I say and zip it with all the questions.

"All done," the stylist says and starts packing up her things.

"Oh my gawd, Fallon! You look amazing," Devya squeals. "Come take a look." She grabs my hand and pulls me into her bathroom which has a full length mirror on the back of the door. I nearly choke when I see myself. The Balmain mini-dressed paired with the six inch stilettos makes me look like I have legs for days. My hair is done up in this cute messy up-do that has a loose, half braid crown that runs along the left side of my head and ends in a loose chignon at the base of my neck with soft tendrils framing my face. My makeup is perfection. The stylist did a killer smoky eye making my green eyes glimmer and pop like never before and the bold red lip she gave me just makes the entire look pop.

"Wow! I love it." I say, just barely above a whisper.

Devya's standing behind me cheesing and looking like a fuck-ing goddess in her dress. "You look so beautiful," I say, turning to face her.

"Thanks boo!" she says and does a little twirl.

Devya's phone vibrates. "The car's here," she says looking at the screen.

Suddenly a whole host of butterflies take flight in my belly. I'm about to walk into a hornet's nest with no protective covering. I have no idea what I'm in for but based on what I've been through at this school so far there's no telling what will happen tonight.

It's about an hour and a half drive to the location where the Dare Party is being held. The car pulls up to a secluded property located at the end of a private road. The property is surrounded by a heavy, black iron gate that opens automatically as our car pulls up.

"You ready?" Devya says as the car comes to a stop in front of a large mansion resembling one of those old southern plantation houses with its box-like shape, huge pillars and large porch that wraps around the house.

"As ready as I'll ever be," I say as a valet opens the car door for us to get out.

As we enter the house Devya and I are greeted by a young man holding a tray of champagne. We each take one and then are led down a hall and into a ballroom. Of course, this house has a ball-room. From what I was able to peek at as we were led to the ball-room, the inside of the mansion is everything you'd expect; an enormous foyer that feeds into a sweeping staircase, beautiful hardwood floors, expensive furnishings and amazing artwork.

The ballroom is elegantly decorated with a series of three large, round tables each with a lovely, ivory table cloth and ex-pensive gold place settings for five. At the front of the room is a long, rectangular table set for nine. All of the pure bloods from

Bradford are already inside chatting and drinking with the exception of Bexley, Harlyn, Alisander and Zade. As we move further into the ballroom I see two freshman boys from Bradford standing off to the side quietly talking. There's a group of kids, two girls and two boys that I don't recognize. They're huddled together whispering and stealing glances at everyone.

"Who are they?" I nod towards the group of kids I don't recognize.

"That's Ariel Underwood, Becca Love, Slade Waldgrave and Hunter Gryffon. They go to Elmsley Academy. You heard of it?"

I shake my head. "No."

"It's about two hours from Bradford. It's another private school shaping the minds of the elite only they don't have half the wealth or power that Bradford students wield. But those four," she nods her head in their direction. "They're families are pretty powerful; lots of money and lots of connections so they get a seat at the table."

"Interesting," I say and take a tiny sip of champagne, the bubbles tickling my nose.

Suddenly, the hairs on the back of my neck stand up and my body goes all warm. I turn to find Lucca staring at me from across the room. He's standing with Indigo, Tatum and Chloe who are huddled together talking but he's focused on me.

I shiver and my body heats in recognition under his gaze.

I've been secretly tutoring Lucca for over a month and all of our sessions have ended with him pressing me against the library door and kissing me breathless. Outside of our tutoring sessions he barely looks at me. No one would suspect that we meet every day to study and make out. I want to tell Devya and Harlyn but I made a promise.

"You okay?" Devya asks, a concerned look on her face.

"I'm fine. Why?"

"You look a little flushed all of a sudden," she says eyeing me.

"It's probably the champagne or nerves or a combination of both. I'm gonna find a bathroom so I can take a minute and get myself together before this thing kicks off."

"I'll go with you," Devya says.

"No, it's fine. I'll be quick. Just point me in the direction of the bathroom."

"There's one down the hall to the left," Devya says.

"Thanks. I'll be right back," I say and head for the bathroom.

The bathroom wasn't hard to find and as I go inside and close the door, Lucca slides his foot in the entry preventing me from closing it.

"What are you doing?" I whisper as he slips inside and shuts the door behind him.

He locks it then turns to me. "Damn, you look good," he says pulling me to him.

Before I can think too hard about it, my hands are sliding up his chest and curling around his neck. He smells of sandalwood and clove, an enchanting mix. And he looks devastatingly handsome in a black snake print, velvet formal jacket, black slacks, white tuxedo shirt and black bowtie. He fingers a loose tendril of my hair as he stares down at me with eyes that are smoldering and hungry. Before I can say anything, his generous mouth is descending on mine and without thinking I slant my head and open my mouth urging him to explore. He doesn't disappoint.

Lucca's mouth is warm and soft and tastes like mint toothpaste. He tightens his hold on me pressing me tighter against his body. His tongue teases and pulls at mine as he takes total control of the kiss. He spins us around so my back is against the door then trails his fingers up my thigh and plays at the skin just below the hem of my dress. Slowly he works his fingers underneath the hem and massages my inner thigh. He slowly moves his hand further up my dress until his fingers are brushing the soft material of my panties.

A desperate moan fills the bathroom and I realize that it's coming from me. Things are getting hot and heavy really fast and there's a ballroom full of people not too far away. As much as I want to stay here wrapped up in Lucca, lost in his kiss, I can't. We can't. Reluctantly, I pull back from the kiss, completely breathless and utterly in need of more. I press the back of my head against the door and look at him.

He's completely wound up and turned on. His eyes are ablaze, his breathing is raw and there's a feral heat wafting from his body surrounding the both of us.

"Shit," he says pressing his body against mine. "I don't know what it is about you but I want you so bad, Fallon."

I lick my lips then tug my bottom lip between my teeth.

"Don't do that," Lucca whispers, his voice shaky. "Unless you want to leave this bathroom a total mess from having me fuck you against the door."

I swallow hard as a new round of heat hits my body and fresh goosebumps appear on my skin. Losing my v-card to Lucca Caldwell is something that's crossed my mind several times since we starting making out on a regular basis but having it go down in the bathroom of some mansion with the rest of the pure bloods not too far away just isn't going to happen.

I press my hands to his chest and gently nudge him back, putting some space between us. "We should get back," I say.

He doesn't move right away. Instead he stands there staring at me, his brown eyes roaming over my body.

"Lucca, come on. We're not having a quickie in the bathroom of some random mansion. I'm not that kind of girl."

He wipes his hand down his face then shoves them in his pockets. "I know, Fallon. And I think that's why I'm so drawn to you. Because you're not that kind of girl. You're not like the rest of the Bradford girls. But, I'm so fucking attracted to you and I know you're attracted to me too."

"I am...it's just..."

He puts a finger to my lips silencing me. "I want you and this thing between us is going to come to a head sooner or later."

He stares down at me for several seconds before placing a soft kiss to my forehead then leaving the bathroom.

I move to the sink curling my fingers around the edge and taking several deep breaths to calm my racing heart. Lucca Caldwell is a force to reckon with. One touch from him and my body goes up in flames.

I look at my reflection in the mirror and frown. My lipstick is smeared all to hell and my dress is crooked. I look utterly brazen and worked over. I yank a few napkins sitting in a neat pile next to the sink and wipe the lipstick from around my mouth then dig in my clutch and pull out the tube of lipstick the stylist left for me to take. I reapply my lipstick, smooth my dress back in place and then head back to the ballroom.

I make it back to find that Bexley, Alisander and Zade have arrived and everyone is seated at one of the three round tables. Lucca's at the table with Chloe, Indigo, Tatum and Harlyn and the two Bradford freshman are seated at the table with the four kids from Elmsley.

All eyes are on me as I make my way into the ballroom.

One of the waiters walks up to me. "You're the last one to be seated. Please follow me," he says and leads me to the table that's slightly in front of the other two and closest to the long, rectangular table at the front of the room.

I stiffen when I see that Bexley is seated at the table. She scowls at me but doesn't say anything.

Devya, Alisander, and Zade are also at the table. There's an empty seat between Zade and Alisander that the waiter pulls out for me. I'm a ball of nerves as I sit down. The heady scent of black licorice and cola fills my nostrils and I close my eyes for a brief moment trying to block out the intoxicating scent. It doesn't work so I tilt away from Zade and lean more towards Alisander. Big mistake. He smells of bergamot and citrus. Very masculine. Very sexy. I grab the glass of water on the table in front of me and gulp it down. These boys will be the death of me.

A bell tinkles somewhere in the room and a side entrance to the ballroom opens and thirteen well-dressed older men and two women enter in a single file line with my grandfather at the front. I press my lips together to conceal my shock. *What the heck is he doing here?*

"Finally," Alisander says barely above a whisper.

I watch as my grandfather leads the line of adults to the long, rectangular table at the front where they all take a seat with my grandfather taking the center-most chair. But he doesn't sit down. He remains standing his eyes surveying the room. He gives me a brief nod as his gaze passes over me.

"Welcome, everyone, to the fortieth annual Dare Party," he says and everyone takes their knife and taps it against their wine glass. Well, everyone but me, that is. I clearly don't know the protocol here.

Devya motions for me to pick up my knife and join in. I do and manage to get in a few taps before everyone stops and places their knife back on the table.

"Represented here tonight are some of the most powerful families in the world and tonight we welcome a few new families into the fold. As always let's start the evening off with roll call," he finishes then sits down.

The man at the far end of the table stands. He's handsome with smooth mahogany skin and a chiseled face. "Darren Caldwell. Represented by my son Lucca Caldwell."

I look at Lucca then back at his father. The resemblance is clear - same mahogany skin, angular jaw and generous mouth.

The woman sitting next to Lucca's father stands up. She has an elegant, almost understated beauty about her. "Alexa North. Represented by my daughter, Chloe North."

One by one the adults at the table stand and give their name and call out their heir's name. Indigo and Tatum's mother is at the table. She's an exotic beauty with dark brown skin and almond shaped, hazel eyes. The man next to her stands and introduces himself as Denton Radcliffe. He looks like a bit of a rock star with his strong jawline and the typical long, shaggy, messy rocker hair. He's clearly the rebel up there much like his daughter Harlyn is at Bradford. Next to him is Nikos Davenport, the father of Alisander. He's tan, handsome and has a charming smile, much like Alisander. Zade's father, Michael Amherst, is next to Mr. Davenport. He's just as dark and brooding as his son and has the same intense blue-violet eyes. Devya's father Raj Nadar, is a thin but very handsome man with the same dark eyes as Devya. The man that stands next him is a little taller than

everybody and the arrogant set of his chin screams, I'm important. I know who he is and who his heir is before he even says the
name Noble Barringer.

After the rest of the adults at the table introduce themselves
my grandfather stands. He looks very distinguished in his dark
blue suite. "I'm Wilson Gamble and I'm proud to be represented
by my granddaughter Fallon Gamble," he says gesturing to me.

All eyes turn to me and all I want to do is shrink down into
my seat and disappear under table. I'm glad when he continues
speaking and introduces the new families attending the dinner
for the first time.

"We have two new families joining us this year. The Martels
and the Fridmans."

The last two men at the table with my grandfather introduce
themselves and announce their heirs as the two freshmen from
Bradford.

After the introductions is a formal dinner. Waiters in white
gloves serve a four course meal of lobster bisque, gilded green
salad, herb crusted lamb with roasted potatoes and a dark chocolate crème brûlée.

"Eat fast assholes so we can get to the real party," Alisander
says finishing off his crème brûlée.

"The real party?" I ask looking over at him.

"Yeah, all this shit here is real formal. After they leave," he
points his thumb at the adult table, "the real party begins. You'll
see."

After everyone finishes eating and the waiters clear the tables
my grandfather stands. "The Dare Party is a long standing tradition and we look to you," he says gesturing to us kids at the
round tables. "To keep our traditions and legacies intact. We expect all of you to do what is necessary to do that," he finishes
looking straight at me.

My heart literally goes into overdrive. My grandfather clearly
has expectations of me that I'm not sure I can meet. I'm barely
surviving at Bradford as it is.

"Now, we will each have a few moments with our heirs and

then we'll leave you all to it," my grandfather says.

I watch as everyone gets up to meet their family member. There are no hugs or soft smiles. It looks as if the adults are preparing the kids for something serious.

I swallow hard as I watch my grandfather approach. "Hi," I say when he reaches me.

"Hello, Fallon. You look well," he says.

"Thank you."

"How are things at Bradford?" he asks, his eyes watching me closely.

"I'm adjusting," I say with a shrug.

He studies me for a moment, his green eyes assessing.

I fidget under his gaze.

"It's a tough crowd you find yourself in now. I know that. But you're a Gamble and while you didn't grow up in this lifestyle, you belong here. It's your birthright. I can't tell you what's going to happen tonight but just know that you'll be tested and it won't be easy. But, no matter what you have to be up for the challenge."

"The challenge?" I ask.

"I can't tell you anything more. Just know that both your father and I attended the Dare Party and we both did what we had to do to secure the family's position. I know you've been through a lot lately. And I know those kids at Bradford have been trying to break you but you're clearly a very strong young woman. You're a Gamble. You'll be fine, Fallon." he says and pats me gently on the shoulder before walking away.

I'm left standing there feeling completely lost and utterly confused.

CHAPTER TWELVE

The ballroom empties out quickly and I'm left standing in the same spot my grandfather left me. I look over to see Devya making her way over to me.

"C'mon, it's time," Devya says grabbing my arm and pulling me towards the exit.

"Time for what?" I ask worried. I can't get what my grandfather said out of my head about me being up for the challenge tonight.

"Time to party. Now that the fuddie-duds are gone, we can cut lose," Devya says with a big smile as she leads me through the mansion.

I can hear the faint sounds of music blaring as we make our way down the hall.

"What up bitches!" Harlyn says as we enter the room where the music is coming from. "Let's get this party started," she says holding up a bottle of vodka and a bag of gummy bears.

"Vodka and gummy bears," I frown.

"Not just any gummy bears, Padawan." She shoves the bottle of vodka in Devya's hands. "Hold this."

Devya just laughs and cradles the bottle to her chest.

Harlyn opens the bag of gummies and takes out three. "Each one of these cute, little bears has fifteen grams of THC and everybody at the party has to take one." She opens her mouth and sits a gummy on her tongue, wiggling it at me and Devya before closing her mouth and eating it. She goes over to Devya who, without a word, opens her mouth and allows Harlyn to place a gummy inside.

My stomach is a ball of nerves right now. I drink a little bit but I've never done drugs, not even weed. "I think I'll pass," I say as Harlyn turns to me, the gummy bear pinched between her forefinger and thumb. She looks over at Devya who now has a slightly nervous look on her face.

"What?" I look from Devya to Harlyn.

"You can't turn down anything from a pure blood at this party, Fallon," Harlyn says her face turning serious.

"Why not?"

"Because that's the way it is. At any point, any person in this room can present you with something to drink, eat, or do. You can't refuse."

"She's right," Devya adds. "Getting through this party deter-mines how the rest of your year goes. Remember what I told you about the consequences of not following through at this party?"

I nod. "Something about being shunned and ridiculed."

"Yeah, but for you, it'll be really bad. So just follow our lead on everything," Devya says motioning to herself and Harlyn.

"Now open up, Square," Harlyn smirks.

Everything in me says this is not a good idea but I open my mouth and allow Harlyn to place the gummy inside.

"Now chew," she says with a laugh.

I chew the gummy which is not at all what I expect weed candy to taste like. It's actually pretty good; very sweet. No weed taste at all.

"Time for some drinks. C'mon," Harlyn says leading us to a bar set up near the back of the room.

All of the kids from dinner are posted up around the room. Lucca, Zade, and Alisander are sitting around a card table with the two Elmsley boys. Chloe and Tatum are sitting on one of the couches whispering and Bexley and Indigo are standing near the bar with Ariel Underwood and Becca Love.

"What's up, cuz?" Harlyn says when we reach the bar.

Bexley turns on us, her perfectly arched brow raised in judge-ment. "I'm good but I see you're still hanging with the trash."

"Jeez, Bex, it's a party. Why don't you lighten up?" Harlyn says.

"Whatever, Harlyn. I don't even know how we're even related," Bexley says with a hair flip and walks away. Indigo and the two Elmsley girls follow behind her.

Harlyn rolls her eyes. "Trust me, I don't know either. I'm so much cooler than she is. Maybe she was adopted."

"Forget her. Pour us some drinks," Devya says.

While I pretend to listen to Harlyn and Devya go back and forth about what drink to make, I eye the boys over at the card table. I don't know what game they're playing but it looks like Alisander might be winning. He's wearing a big, cocky grin while the rest of the boys are scowling.

Lucca looks up and sees me watching. Our eyes lock and his scowl flattens, his eyes darken and the corners of his mouth turn up slightly. I can feel the heat of his gaze to my core. Memories of us in the bathroom locked together in a heated kiss come flooding back and my mouth waters. Like literally waters.

Zade looks at Lucca then over his shoulder at me, his blue-violet eyes penetrating. He runs his tongue over his mouth and it's like I can feel the caress of it on my own lips. Without thinking I bring my fingers to my mouth running them gently across my bottom lip. I look from Zade to Lucca and find myself trapped between the heat of both their gazes. I can't help the shortness of breath or the tightness in my belly. What the hell is going on? Has the weed candy already kicked in? Because I'm over here trippin'. I got two very different boys getting me worked up at the same damn time. *What is my life right now?*

"Listen up everyone," Bexley says. She's standing in the middle of the room looking like a fucking evil goddess in her gold sequined mini dress. "A bunch of kids from Bradford and Elmsley will be arriving soon so let's get the reason we're here out of the way so we can really get this party started." Bexley holds a silver tray in her hand and on that tray are sixteen envelops. "On this tray lies this year's dares. For those of you who are new to this, there are sixteen envelops with each of our names on one of them. You must complete whatever task is written on the piece of paper inside the envelope...if you dare. The task must be completed before sun up." She turns her holier than thou gaze on me. "If you fail to complete your dare, you're fined a hundred thousand dollars, you'll be shunned by everyone for the rest of the year and most importantly you'll prove to your family what a disgrace you are."

Alisander gets up from the table and grabs Bexley around the waist. "Alright Bex, enough with the theatrics. Just hand out the envelopes."

Bexley smiles sweetly up at him. "Sure thing, babe. Since you're already up, go ahead and grab yours," she says holding the stray out to him.

Alisander grabs his envelope then goes back to his seat at the card table.

"Lucca, you're next," Bexley says.

Lucca grabs his envelope and opens it right away and reads it. His features tighten and he cuts his eyes at me before he goes back and sits at the table.

One by one Bexley calls everyone up to grab their envelope. She saves me for last.

"Stray...I mean, Fallon. You're up," She says, a plastic smile on her face.

I make my way to Bexley, all eyes are on me. No one's talking or moving. It feels like I'm walking the plank or something.

Bexley narrows her eyes and purses her lips in that haughty way of hers as she holds the tray out to me. I grab the last envelope then hurry away to stand next to Harlyn.

Bexley holds the tray up showing everyone that there are no envelopes left. "The sun is set to rise at six-thirty tomorrow. We are all to meet in the media room at that time to get an accounting of who succeeded and who failed. Until then, let's party bitches."

"Hell yeah," Alisander says and heads to the bar and grabs a bottle of tequila. "Bottle shots. Line up assholes."

Everyone gets in line and opens their mouth.

"C'mon," Harlyn says grabbing my elbow and guiding me over to the line.

"Harlyn, I can't. I already ate an edible and now shots. I'm gonna be wasted within the hour," I fret.

"It's cool. Me and Devya, we got you. Fallon, you have to do this. No refusing, remember. And besides, you're gonna need some liquid courage once you read what's inside that envelope," Harlyn says then tilts her head back and opens her mouth.

Alisander pours a decent shot into her mouth then moves to me. His eyes roam over my body before they settle on my face. "Not bad, Fallon. You do clean up nicely, don't you? I'mma find you later. Now open up."

I open my mouth and Alisander hooks his finger under my chin and tilts my head back then pours a stream of tequila down my throat. I put my hands up signaling enough but Alisander just laughs and keeps pouring. Unable to take anymore, I close my mouth and the liquid drips down my lips and chin.

"Let me get that for you," Alisander says and runs his tongue up my chin and across my mouth.

"Hey," I say pressing my hands to his chest and pushing him back.

He just laughs and tips the bottle to his own lips and takes a big swig.

I look over to see Bexley scowling at me.

"I think Alisander may have the hots for you, Fallon," Devya says.

"I think all the boys have the hots for our girl," Harlyn says with a wink.

"What? No way. They all despise me," I argue.

"Maybe in public but I've seen the way they look at you. If they get you alone you're in trouble." Harlyn says shaking her head.

I'll never admit it but she's right. Hell, I've already made out with Lucca numerous times and if Alisander puts his mouth on me again I know I won't push him away. And let's not even talk about Zade. Everything in me wants to know Zade Amherst intimately.

"Well, it's a good thing you guys will be by my side all night," I say, plastering a big, cheesy grin on my face.

Harlyn and Devya laugh.

"So," I say holding my up my envelope. "Shall we see what's in these?"

"There's time for that later. Right now, let's have some fun," Devya says.

"Don't you want to know what's in your envelope?" I ask.

"Listen here, eager beaver, once you open that envelope your entire night will change so we like to have a little fun first. Trust me, you want to wait a little bit before opening that," Harlyn says pointing to the envelope in my hand.

"Okay, fine" I say, giving in. "I'm going to run to the bathroom then I'll be back to party with ya'll."

"Hurry up," Devya says then pulls Harlyn towards the bar.

As I make my way out of the party room, several kids I recognize from Bradford are making their way down the hallway. Surprisingly, they walk right past me without a shoulder brush or derogatory word.

Just before I make it to the bathroom, I'm pulled into one of the rooms lining the hallway. It's dark and I can barely make out anything.

"What the hell?" I yelp.

"It's just me," a deep, velvety voice says.

"Lucca?"

"Yeah," he says turning on the light.

"What are you doing? Did you pull me in here to make out again?"

"Why would you say that?" he asks, disappointment clouding his brown eyes.

"I don't know," I shrug. "It's what we do, right? Make out behind closed doors so no one sees."

Lucca runs his hand down his face. "I just don't want everybody all up in our business."

"Or, you don't want anybody to know that you been messing around with the stray," I say, lifting my chin in defiance. I'm feeling really bold right now. Could it be the weed? Maybe the booze?

"It's not like that, Fallon," he says.

"Really? Then tell me how it is, Lucca," I counter.

Lucca closes his eyes, tilts his head back and lets out a deep sigh. "It's complicated. But, I do like you, Fallon."

A blanket of warmth wraps around me at his words and I relax a little. "I like you too," I say. "Honestly, you've given me the least amount of shit since I started at Bradford. And getting to know you during our tutoring sessions has actually been kind of cool. You're a pretty decent guy, Lucca Caldwell."

He drops his head and lets out a cynical little laugh. "You may not think that after what I'm about to tell you."

That warm feeling starts to fade and is replaced by nausea and nerves as I stare at him. "Tell me what?"

He wrings his hands together nervously and looks away.

Now I'm getting nervous. "Lucca, what is it?"

He scrubs his hand down his face and lets out a deep sigh. "So, I was invited to football camp at Texas A&M over the summer. I was dumb excited about it. I had a great season at Bradford. I was at the top of my game but..." he walks over to stand by the dresser, putting a lot of space between us.

"But what?"

"Those guys at camp, they were off the charts talented. I had a hard time keeping up so I did something bad. Something that if it gets out, will ruin my football career before it even gets started."

I walk over to Lucca, press my hands lightly to his chest and stare up at him. "It's okay, you don't have to tell me."

He holds up the little gold piece of paper. "Yes, I do. I have to tell everyone."

I look at the paper then back at Lucca. He looks so scared and sad. "It's okay. Whatever you did, I won't judge you. And I'll never tell anyone."

I can feel the thundering of his heart against my hand and I know whatever he's about to confess is serious.

He turns his head away as he if can't bear to look at me. "I took steroids to enhance my performance."

My mouth drops open in shock. That's some major shit. He's

right, if it gets out that he took performance enhancing drugs, his football career is over.

"Are you still taking them?" I ask.

He doesn't respond. Instead, he drops his head in shame.

"Well you have to stop taking them," I say.

"It's not that simple, Fallon," he says, turning his back to me.

I grab his shoulder pulling him back to face me. "Why not? You don't want to end your football career before it starts, do you?"

"Of course, I don't but since I been taking them I've been faster and stronger at practice. Coach is saying a lot of colleges are looking at me. My Dad's got college reps coming to the games to check me out. Things are really good on the field and my pops, he's finally proud of me."

"I get that but, Lucca, if the NCAA finds out that you've been doping, it'll all be for nothing. And what would your Dad say if he found out?"

"He'd probably disown me," he says, shaking his head.

I wrap my arms around Lucca's neck and press my forehead to his. "I know you want to make your Dad proud but you can't do it like this. Steroids are not the answer. They're crazy harmful for your body. I believe in you, Lucca. You don't need steroids to be good at football. It's clear that you love the game and you'll do whatever it takes to succeed at it. I know that if you work hard and push yourself that you can continue to be the best without the steroids."

Lucca wraps his arms around my waist and presses me tightly to him. "Maybe...and I do wanna stop," he starts.

"I'll do what I can to help you," I say before he can offer up a reason not to stop.

Lucca grabs my face between his hands, his brown eyes search my green ones. "Why couldn't I have met you sooner? You're a good person, Fallon. You don't belong here with us. We're not good people."

"Don't say that. You're a good person. I know it. You just made a bad choice."

"I've made many bad choices since I been at Bradford. And all because I want to make my father proud. But you, you're still pure. You're still good. Try not to lose that," he finishes then kisses me softly on the mouth.

CHAPTER THIRTEEN

I'm more than nervous to open my envelope after what just happened with Lucca. Cleary, this Dare Party is not a game.

I stare down at my red polished toes that peek out beyond the thin black strap laid across the top of my feet as I pace the small length of the bathroom, my envelope clenched tightly in my fist. "What could possibly be on this paper," I say aloud. "I don't have any crazy skeletons in my closet. Nothing shameful to confess." I stop pacing and open my hand, the weight of the envelope heavy in my palm. "Just open it, Fallon."

I take a deep breath and quickly unfold the gold piece of paper. I'm thoroughly confused when I see what's on it.

We dare you to work with Zade Amherst to complete your task. Seek him out to find out what your task is.

"What the hell?" Nerves race through my body at the thought of talking to Zade let alone having to work with him. And the note doesn't even say what the task is. This is totally fucked. I know that Devya and Harlyn wanted to get some party time in but there's no way I'll be able to enjoy myself. I'll be too busy watching Zade and wondering what it is that we're supposed to do. "Harlyn and Devya will just have to wait," I say and make my way to find Zade.

The party's in full swing when I get back. It's a scene straight out of a teen movie. The room is packed with rambunctious kids drinking, smoking, dancing and really just cutting up in general. Harlyn and Devya are huddled in a corner smoking weed with Cord Michelson and some girl I don't recognize. Bexley's holding court with Tatum, Chloe and a group of girls from Bradford. Indigo's not with them which is odd since her and Bexley are practically tied at the hip.

I finally spot Zade in the very back of the room leaning against the wall looking bored while he sips a beer. I make a beeline for him but Alisander cuts me off before I reach him.

"Come with me," Alisander says grabbing my hand and pulling me in the opposite direction of where Zade is.

"Wait, I need to talk to Zade," I say trying to pull my hand out of his and ignoring the tingly sensation generated from our connecting hands.

"This won't take long," he says leading me out of the party, down the hall and up the stairs.

"Where are we going?"

"Some place quiet," he says, finally stopping when we reach what looks to be a game room.

There's a pool table in the middle of the space and arcade style video games all around the room. I haven't seen this entire house but what I've seen so far is beyond impressive.

"Fine, it's quiet here. What's up?" I ask pulling my hand out of his.

He stares at me for a few seconds before running his hand through his flaxen colored locks. "You're really pretty, Fallon. You know that?"

I shift nervously under his scrutiny. "Thanks."

He moves in, closing the distance between us. "This world of ours that you've entered into is pretty fucked up. But I'm sure you already know that."

"It's definitely different from where I come from."

"I bet you were a good person back in Nebraska," he says fingering a tendril of hair near my temple.

"I was and I still am," I say.

He looks at me his eyes deadpan. "You won't be after tonight," he says then leans down and presses his lips to mine.

The kiss is gentle. His lips are warm and soft against mine. I should probably pull back but I don't. I like this feel of his mouth on mine. I want more.

Alisander places one hand at my waist and kneads the flesh there and brings his other hand to the back of my neck gently caressing the delicate skin with his fingertips. I lean into him and open my mouth inviting him to taste and explore every inch of my mouth and he doesn't disappoint. Alisander takes his time sweeping his tongue in my mouth, running it over my teeth and cheeks before swirling it around my tongue. Being kissed by Alisander is like being lost in space. Time doesn't exist. Only the moment of being swept up in his embrace and captivated by the masterful way he kisses.

"I'm sorry," he says pulling back. "But I had to do that one good time because after I say what I have to say to you, I may not get the chance to do it again."

I'm breathless and a tad discombobulated from his kiss to respond right away.

Alisander moves away from me and leans against the pool table. He pulls out his envelope and holds it out. "If you don't understand the point of tonight and these envelopes now, you will by the end of the night."

"What do you mean?"

"I mean that everything we do and say tonight is all about survival in the long run."

"I don't understand," I say moving to stand in front of him.

"It's all about leverage, Fallon. In a few years, we'll be the ones running our families businesses. Calling the shots. Making deals. Using information to get what we want."

"I would never do that?" I say with conviction.

He shakes his head and lets out a little chuckle. "That's what you say now but you'll be just like the rest of us. Doing whatever it takes to preserve your family legacy."

There's a sadness about him as I watch him now. I can see the burden of his family weighing heavy on him. I go to him and place my hand over his. "We don't have to be like everyone else, you know."

"It's too late for me. I'm already like the rest of them which is why," he removes his hand from mine and drops his head. "I must confess that last summer I was out drinking and partying all night and I crashed my car."

"That's not all that bad of a confession, Alisander."

"Wait for it," he says holding up a finger. "I crashed my car and killed some poor kid who was dumb enough to get in the car with me. His name was Danny Fields. And before you ask, I didn't even get so much as a slap on the wrist. My family took care of everything."

My hand flies to my mouth. WTF?! Did he just confess to manslaughter? "Are you serious?"

"Yeah, and now you have leverage on me," he says, his face hardening.

"I don't want leverage on you, Alisander. You just confessed to being responsible for some poor kid's death. That has to weigh heavy on you. Why would I want to add to that?"

He doesn't say anything. He just stands there with his head down.

"You know what I want?" I say to him.

He shakes his head but doesn't look at me.

"I want you to be okay," I say.

He looks up then, a touch of a smile gracing the corners of his mouth. He walks over to me and runs his thumb along my cheek and the spot where he touches heats and tingles. "Like I said, you're a good person."

"What the fuck, Alisander!" Bexley yells as she enters the game room.

Alisander drops his hand and shoves it in his pocket. "What are you doing up here with her and why in the hell are you touching her?" Bexley scowls as she brushes past me.

"I was just handling a little business," he says holding up his envelope.

"So, you told her?" Bexley asks.

Alisander nods.

Bexley whips around fixing her steely blue gaze on me. "I may not be able to touch you tonight but just know I'm ready to fuck your world up the minute you fail to do what's in your envelope."

"Who says I'm gonna fail," I say, stiffening my spine.

"You don't have the nuts to hang in our world so I know you'll fail."

"Say what you want, Bexley but you have no idea who I am. You've been trying to break me since I came to this school. You haven't yet and you never will."

"We'll see about that," Bexley says and with a toss of her hair she turns back to Alisander. "Come do shots with me."

Alisander doesn't say anything he just walks out of the game room.

"Stay away from Alisander. He's mine," Bexley hisses on her way out.

She really is an asshole, I think as I leave the game room and once again seek out Zade. Turns out I don't have to go too far. He's sitting at the bottom of the steps talking to Harlyn.

"Where the fuck have you been, chic?" Harlyn yells up the steps, her speech a bit slurred. "Devya and I were waiting for you at the bar for forever."

"My bad. I had to take care of something," I say.

"And now you have to go with Zade," she says pointing at him.

"Go where?" I ask looking from her to Zade.

Zade holds up his envelope. "We should get this over with."

"Get what over with?" I ask pulling out my envelope. "All mine says is that I need to work with you to complete my task."

"Exactly. Let's go," he says and starts walking down the hall.

"Come with us," I say to Harlyn.

"Sorry kitty-cat but I can't. This is you and Zade's thing. But I'll be here when you get back. I'll probably be fucked up but I'll be here," she says bracing her hands on my shoulders.

"Fine," I say with a sigh and turn to follow Zade.

"Hold up," Harlyn says spinning me back around. "You good?

Has the gummy kicked in yet?"

"I'm not sure. Maybe. I mean, I don't feel any different unless being high on weed gummies give me the courage to say some things I normally wouldn't."

Harlyn laughs. "Could be. Cannabis effects everyone differently. Just be sure to ride the high when it really kicks in. Okay."

"Yeah, okay," I say even though I don't have the faintest clue what she's talking about.

"Let's go," Zade calls from down the hall.

"I'll find you when I get back," I say to Harlyn then jog down the hall to catch up with Zade.

I follow him outside and over to a black Icon Sheen motorcycle. It's sleek, beautiful and looks extremely powerful. There's a black helmet hanging from the handlebars. Zade grabs it and hands it to me.

"Put this on," he orders.

I take the helmet but don't put it on. I need to know what's going on and where he plans on taking me. "Where are we going?"

He hops on the bike then looks over at me. "To do what it says in my envelope. Now get on," he commands as he revs up the engine.

There's something about the way he's looking at me. His blue-violet eyes are hard as stone and daring me to defy him. It's a total turn-on. I put the helmet on and hop on the back of the bike, wrapping my arms loosely around his waist. Licorice and cola invade my nostrils overtaking my senses. I press my body into him and the hard ridges of his back against the soft flesh of my front is a whole other experience.

"Hold on tight," Zade says then takes off.

He must be going well over a hundred miles an hour as we speed down the long country road leading from the mansion and he doesn't let up as he hits the highway zig-zagging between cars. The wind feels like heaven against my skin. It's like a thousand tiny fingers massaging me. The sensation is intoxicating.

We drive for a good fifteen minutes before Zade exits the highway and turns down a long country road. There's no traffic. It's just us speeding down the road. It's dark but I can make out fields of vineyards on either side of the road.

Zade slows down and pulls over to the side of the road.

"C'mon," he says, hopping off the bike then grabs my hand and helps me off.

The touch of Alisander's hand on mine gave me tingles but Zade's touch...Zade's touch is a lightning bolt. I'm shocked and frozen in place as electricity races through my entire body.

Zade's haunting gaze travels from our connected hands, up my arm and lands on my face. I stare back at him, not breathing. How can I breathe when my body is firing on all cylinders and I'm lost in the hard edges of those blue-violet eyes? There's a connection between us. I feel it and I know he does too.

"Helmet," he says, releasing my hand.

Even though he's no longer touching me, a current of hot volts still run through my body. I can't just stand here staring at him. I gotta get it together. I slowly release the breath I'm holding and pull the helmet off and hand it to him. "Where are we?" I ask, my voice a bit shaky.

"On the outskirts of Calais Creek Vineyards," he says and starts walking towards the rows of grapevines.

I follow after him. "Why are we here?"

"Because this is where we complete the task in the envelope," he says.

I move after him, my stilettos a major hindrance in my ability to keep up. I quickly slip them off and jog after him.

"Will you wait up a second please!" I call after him.

Of course, he doesn't stop.

"Zade!" I shout.

"What?" He barks, whipping around and fixing his steely blue-violet gaze on me. There it is. That look of discontent he normally wears is back.

I shrink back a little. "I just want to know what's going on. All the paper in my envelope said was to work with you to complete my task. It doesn't say what the task is. What does your paper say?"

He doesn't answer. He just pulls his envelope out his pocket and hands it to me. I'm shocked when I open it and read what's on the paper.

"We have to set fire to this vineyard?" I stare at him in disbelief.

"Yes, and keep your voice down," he growls.

"We can't do this. It's a crime. We'll be in so much trouble if we get caught," I fret.

"Then we better not get caught," Zade says and moves alongside the fence surrounding the vineyard as if he's looking for something.

I stay where I'm at and watch him. I feel utterly sick to my stomach. I've never committed a crime in my life. Not so much as steal a pack of gum and now I'm expected to commit arson? This is nuts.

"Here it is," Zade says picking up a big, black duffle bag. He opens it pulling out cans of gasoline and matches. He holds a can of gasoline out to me.

"What am I supposed to do with that?" I ask looking at him like he's crazy.

"Use it to set this bitch on fire, duh," Bexley says from behind me. Her voice as arrogant and haughty as always.

I whip around. What the hell is she doing here and when did she arrive? I didn't hear a car pull up but sure enough parked on the side of the road is a silver Aston Martin One-77.

"Hand me that gas can so we can get this over with and get back to the party," she says walking over to Zade who hands her a gas can.

He picks up another one and holds it out to me. "We need to hurry. You guys start here. Just pour gas over everything. I'll go up there and do the same," he says, pointing a few yards up.

I look at them both like they've lost their minds. "This is crazy. We can't do this," I say not taking the gas can from Zade.

Bexley cock's a brow, smirks and shakes her head at me. "Like I said, you don't have the nuts."

"You know what," I say turning on Bexley, "I been trying to lay low. Stay away from you. Let you continue to sit on your paper throne at Bradford but you make it really hard because you take every opportunity to be a bitch to me," I spit.

Bexley's full lips tighten into a flat line and her aqua colored eyes darken. "That's because you don't belong here, Stray," she says stalking towards me. "You're nothing but a pathetic little bastard whose grandfather is -"

"Enough!" Zade shouts cutting Bexley off and moves to stand between the two of us. He closes his eyes and lets out a rough, deep sigh. "Look, we have to do this. No ifs, ands or buts about it." He fixes his gaze on me. "I know you already talked to Lucca and Alisander so you know the deal. Everything we do is calculated. It serves some purpose that will more than likely benefit one or all of our families at some point down the road."

"But what we're being asked to do is crazy. It's criminal."

"Then don't participate. Sit your lame ass down over there and watch the big kids work. You're not cut out for the life we live anyway. We all know it so nobody will be surprised that you don't complete your dare," Bexley sneers.

"C'mon, Bex, that's enough," Zade says his eyes still on me. "She's right, though. You don't have to do this, but, Fallon, if you don't there will be major repercussions for you and your family."

"I know. I'll be shunned and ridiculed for the rest of the year. But that's nothing. I've been pretty much treated that way since I came to Bradford," I finish, shooting daggers at Bexley.

"Okay, so you can handle it. I get it. But what about your grandfather?" Zade says, his face serious, his eyes questioning.

"What about him?"

"You not completing your dare is detrimental not just to you but to your grandfather as well. He will lose his position within our circle."

"A position he doesn't deserve anyway," Bexley mumbles.

I ignore the hateful wench and move closer to Zade. "Are you saying that if I don't help burn down this vineyard I'll make trouble for my grandfather?" I ask in disbelief.

"That's exactly what I'm saying. The things we do are for family. You weren't raised how we were. From the time I was born my parents beat me over the head with the idea that the Amherst name is everything. It means everything and we do what is necessary to protect it. Your grandfather has more wealth than a lot of our families combined but he lost his heir so his pull within the inner circle was tenuous until you came along. The bastard daughter of his dead son."

My heart constricts at his words. Not because they're not true but because they're hard to hear out loud. I never thought of myself as a bastard. Just a girl raised by her mother because her father died before she was born.

"Look, I don't mean to be harsh but someone like you would normally be kept hidden and certainly not allowed to be brought into the inner circle. But your grandfather changed the game. He legitimized you and took back absolute control of the power within the circle. So, if you want to ruin your family name and have your grandfather lose what he just gained back, don't help us. Just stand there while we spill the gas and light the match."

"I don't know why you're wasting your time trying to convince her, Zade. She's not one of us. Let's just you and me get this over with." Bexley says and proceeds to douse the nearest set of vines with gasoline.

CHAPTER FOURTEEN

I never imagined I'd find myself here. Standing on the side of a country road, barefoot trying to decide whether or not to set fire to a vineyard. I mean honestly, this is nuts.

Bexley's already disappeared down a row of grapevines covering them with gasoline. Zade's standing a few feet away from me, head cocked, hands shoved into his pockets, watching me. Waiting for me to decide.

What I really want to do is rewind time. Go back to when my mom was healthy. Back to a time when my biggest decision was deciding what outfit to wear. Those were simpler times. Now I'm being asked to commit a crime to not only save myself from a year of further torture but to also help secure my grandfather's place in some elite secret society. A grandfather I barely know. A grandfather who is the only family I have left. He took me in and now he's banking the family name on me. Talk about pressure. I know what I'm being asked to do is wrong. I know it is. But what choice do I have?

"Fine. I'll do it." I say and as I speak the words I swear I see a spark of disappointment in Zade's eyes.

"Alright then. Let's do this," he says and picks up two gasoline cans and starts dousing grapevines.

I grab a gas can, my hands trembling as I lift it and walk over to a row of grapevines. I can't believe I'm about to do this. I look over at Zade. He's already halfway down the row splashing gasoline on everything in his path. I take a deep breath and mimic his actions. We move through row after row dousing the grapevines with gasoline until all of the gas cans are empty.

"That's all of it," Zade says. "Let's go." He motions for us to follow him out of the vineyard.

We stand at the edge of a vineyard just staring at it for a few seconds then Zade pulls out matches. I watch as he takes a few from the box and with one strike sets them ablaze. He bends down and drops them into the trail of gasoline leading into the vineyard. The trail erupts into a blue-orange flame that quickly grows and spreads its fingers out to the vines we doused with gasoline. They catch fire immediately lighting up the night.

"See you back at the party, Zade," Bexley says then saunters off. She gets in her car and speeds off without a backward glance.

"We have to go," Zade says packing the gas cans back in the duffle bag and moving quickly over to his motorcycle.

I run after him. "We're taking that with us?"

"If we leave it here somebody will find it," he says grabbing the helmet and handing it to me.

"Wouldn't it have made more sense to have Bexley take this in her car?" I ask.

"Yeah, but as you can see Bex isn't the type to stick around for cleanup. Get on the bike. You'll have to hold this on your lap," he orders.

I give him my best are you crazy look. "How the hell am I supposed to hold a big ass duffle bag on my lap on a motorcycle?"

"Get on," Zade commands, his voice low and deep. His blue-violet eyes piercing.

I obey. What else can I do when he looks at me like that? Besides, I just helped him set fire to a vineyard and I really don't want to get caught.

He sits the duffle bag on my lap then hops on the bike.

"Press your body into the bag so it's squished between the two of us then wrap your arms around me," he instructs.

I do as he says and it's a bit awkward but the duffle bag is secure between our bodies. I'm clutching my fancy stilettos against Zade's stomach trying not to drop them.

Zade revs up the motorcycle and speeds off. He drives a bit slower this time. Maybe because he's worried the duffle bag will fall if he goes too fast.

As soon as we get back to the mansion Zade grabs the duffle bag and disappears. He doesn't say one word to me. He just hops off the bike, grabs the duffle bag and disappears behind the back of the mansion. You'd think a guy would at least say something to you after you committed a crime together.

Bexley's silver Aston Martin is parked haphazardly in the driveway. Almost like she stopped the car and jumped out, not really caring that the car was half on the driveway and half on the grass. But why would she care? This girl thinks the world revolves around her.

I get off the bike and hang the helmet on the handlebars. I stare down at my feet which are covered in dirt. I have to get to a bathroom.

I make my way into the house and spot Devya right away. She's posted up in the hallway with Cord Michelson. She's leaning against the wall, a red solo cup hovering at her lips as she giggles at something Cord is saying.

"You're back," Devya squeals as I pass them.

"Yep," I say.

"Cord and I were just talking about Winter Break. Most of us go to Aspen. Well, all of the pure bloods go for sure which includes you now," she finishes with a big smile.

Cord shifts his gaze towards me, his eyes rounded in surprise.

"The Stray's going to Aspen?"

"Cord, don't you dare call her that," Devya says swatting him on the shoulder. "She's a Gamble. Her grandfather is Wilson Gamble."

"I know that but Bexley said we all have to call her The Stray," he says with a frown.

"Well, after tonight Bexley Barringer will no longer rule this school. Things are changing. You need to be nice to Fallon. Besides, she's my friend and it'll really please me if you're nice to her," Devya says and tweaks his nose.

"Whatever you say, D," Cord says, his mouth splitting into a sexy grin.

"Okay, time for me to move around. I need to clean up." I say, definitely not trying to stick around while Devya and Cord make googly eyes at each other.

"Clean up?" Devya says giving me a once over. Her eyes bug out when she sees how dirty my feet are. "Where the hell have you been?"

"Long story. I'll fill you in later. I need to get to the bathroom," I say.

As I start to move down the hall my cell phone buzzes. It's a text message from an unknown number. I open it and my mouth nearly hits the floor in shock. It's a video of Headmaster Cromwell in his underwear, hogtied, gagged and being spanked by a woman whose head is cut out of the video.

I spin around and look at Devya whose staring at her phone, eyes wide. I walk back over to where her and Cord are. He doesn't have his phone out and he's looking at Devya expectantly.

"Did you just get...?" I start but Devya cuts me off.

"I did. Come here," she says grabbing my arm and pulling me to the side. "Make sure you keep a copy of this video somewhere that only you have access to and you can't tell anyone about it."

"Did all the pure bloods get this video?" I ask.

"Yes, and none of us will talk about it outside of the group. That's very important, Fallon."

"Okay, but this is crazy. Why would we need an incriminating video of Headmaster Cromwell?"

"How do you think we get away with all the crap that we do at Bradford?" Devya asks.

"I figured it was because your parents paid for most of the buildings and basically own the school."

"That's part of it but it doesn't hurt to have something on the Headmaster for insurance," she says with a wink.

"Did one of the pure bloods do this?" I ask already knowing the answer.

Devya nods and shows me her phone. The message came from Indigo James. Of course, the sender showed up as unknown on my phone seeing how the only phone numbers I have are Devya and Harlyn's.

"We each have a task tonight. You completed yours, right?" she asks worry marring her pretty face.

"Yes," I say on a sigh.

"Are the filthy feet a result of it?" She asks wagging her finger at my feet.

"Yep," I nod.

"Well I'm just glad you actually completed your dare. I was a little worried you wouldn't go through with it."

"Do you know what I had to do?" I ask.

"Yeah," Devya nods. "And I'm pretty sure it was hard for you."

"You have no idea. I helped destroy someone's property tonight. Probably ruined their livelihood."

Devya wraps her arm around my shoulder. "Sometimes we have to do difficult things. Things we aren't proud of but it's all in the name of family. And what you did tonight helped to secure your family's place in this circle. It's official, you're one of us now."

"The price of being one of you is pretty high. I have a feeling it's going to take a lot of mental currency for me to stay in this circle."

"It's not all bad, Fallon. I mean we do what we have to do when we have to do it but most of the time it's just kids having fun. You know - partying and shopping."

"I guess. I need to get to the bathroom and clean up." I say.

"I'll go with you," Devya says.

"What about Cord?" I ask, looking at him over my shoulder.

Devya turns to Cord, a sweet smile on her face. "I'm gonna hang with Fallon for a bit. I find you later."

"Alright," Cord says with a shrug like it's no big deal but there's a hint of disappointment in his eyes.

Devya doesn't seem to notice as she loops her arm in mine and pulls me down the hall towards the bathroom.

"So Harlyn told me that you rode with Zade on his bike to the vineyard," Devya says, a mischievous glint in her eyes.

I'm sitting on the edge of the tub with my feet dangling under the faucet. The dirt from the vineyard turning the water a murky brown as it goes down the drain.

"Yeah and he drives like a maniac. Is it a requirement that every Bradford kid do a hundred on the highway?"

Devya laughs. "Bradford kids do everything fast. So, how was it?"

"How was what?" I ask as I scrub the bottom of my feet.

"Riding on the back of Zade's bike? You're the first girl he's ever let get on that thing."

"Really?" I say, grabbing a towel off the rack and drying my feet off.

"Oh yeah. Zade loves that bike. His grandfather gave it to him right before he died. I think it's really special to him."

"Why? Were he and his grandfather close?"

"Yeah. His grandfather left the entire Amherst fortune to Zade but he's a minor so his father has control over everything until Zade turns twenty-one."

"Do he and his father get along?" I ask.

"Not really. I think his father is jealous of the relationship Zade had with his grandfather. At least that's the rumor. Zade doesn't talk about his family. In fact, Zade doesn't talk all that much really. You done?" Devya asks looking at my now clean feet.

"Yeah."

"Good. Let's go find Harlyn," Devya says.

"Just let me put my shoes on," I say slipping into my stilettos.

Devya and I make our way back to the room where the party is in full swing. We weave through the throng of dancing kids and make our way over to the bar in search of Harlyn but she's not there. We sweep the room looking for her but she's nowhere to be found.

"She must be off handling her business," Devya says grabbing a bottle of vodka and pouring some in her cup. "You want a drink?" She asks holding the bottle out to me.

"Nah, I'm good," I say, shaking my head.

"Well let's dance then," Devya says wiggling her shoulders.

"Fine," I laugh and let her lead me to the middle of the room where the rest of the kids are crowded together dancing.

She leads us deep into the crowd of gyrating bodies and we join in swaying our bodies and gyrating our hips. After a while I'm so caught up in the music and dancing that all thoughts of Bradford, the pure bloods and the terrible thing I did earlier all seem to fade away.

"What up bitches!" Harlyn says as she makes her way over to us.

"Where have you been?" I ask.

She pauses, tilts her head and purses her lips at me before holding up her cell phone and tapping.

"What does that mean?" I ask.

"Check your email," she says with a grin.

Both Devya and I pull out our cell phones and check our emails.

"What the hell?" I blurt out. In my email is a copy of the midterm test for every one of my classes.

"You're welcome," Harlyn says and starts moving her body to the music.

Devya laughs and gives her a high-five. Me, on the other hand, I'm a little panicked. We can get in a lot of trouble if anyone finds out we have the midterm tests.

I move in close to Harlyn. "Did you do this?" I whisper.

She nods, her mouth splitting into a shit eating grin. She grabs my hand and spins me around then pulls me into her.

"We all had to do something tonight. This was my something."

"How did you even do that? The midterm for every class? Doesn't the school have that stuff on lockdown?"

"They do but I'm pretty good with computers and Chloe North is even better with them than me so between the two of us it was a piece of cake," she says.

"So, you and Chloe had to work together to complete your task like me and Zade did?"

"Yep. But don't forget Bexley. She helped to.

My eyes automatically roll at the mention of Bexley.

"C'mon, enough with the talking. Let's dance," Harlyn says then steps back and starts doing that damn floss dance that I hate.

"You're nuts," I say with a laugh.

Harlyn just smirks and keeps dancing.

I grab Devya and pull her over and the three of us shake our buns for the next hour.

"Hey, is something going on between you and Lucca?" Harlyn asks.

"What? Why are you asking me that?"

"Because he's been staring at you all night. And he's all eyes on you right now too," she says and nods her chin in his direction.

I look over and sure enough Lucca's posted up against the wall while some girl grinds her ass against him. She's really into it, but Lucca, he's focused on me.

"See what I mean," Harlyn says. "Caitlyn Folgers is all up in his shit and he only has eyes for you."

"Lucca Caldwell doesn't give two shits about me," I say, rolling my eyes. I'm putting on a good front for Harlyn but my insides are like jelly. The way Lucca's watching me has my blood boiling hot. I'd really like to waltz over there and grab Caitlyn Folgers by the hair and drag her away from Lucca.

"Yeah, okay," Harlyn says, her voice dripping with sarcasm.

"Hey, I'll be back," Devya says and takes off.

"Wait," I call after her. "Where are you going?"

"Probably dare business," Harlyn says. "Come on," she grabs my hand and pulls me through the crowd.

"Where are we going?" I ask.

"I wanna smoke," she says and leads me out of the room, down the hall and onto the terrace at the back of the house.

The terrace is large and overlooks a lake. It's a beautiful sight with the moon shining down and reflecting off the water. We take a seat on the loungers facing the water. I watch as Harlyn pulls out a blunt and fires it up. The piney skunk scent floats in the air and invades my nostrils. Harlyn takes two hits and offers it to me.

"Nah, I'm good," I say waving her off.

"You're such a square, Nebraska," Harlyn says with a smirk.

"What happened to Stray?" I ask.

"You're one of us now so I'm giving you a new nickname, Nebraska," she says nodding her head and smiling like she just came up with the best nickname in the world.

Nebraska's not a nickname I'd pick for myself but anything is better than Stray. "If you say so," I say with a shrug.

"I do say so and it'll catch on. Trust me. I can be very persuasive," she says with a wink then takes another pull on the blunt.

"Let me hit that."

I don't have to turn around to recognize that voice. The raspy tenor plays at my ears and sends goosebumps up my arms. I look over to see Zade coming towards us, his raven hair rustling slightly in the wind. He looks at me through hooded eyes as he approaches. I wonder if he'll say anything to me. I haven't seen him since he disappeared earlier with the duffle bag.

Of course, he says nothing so I quietly watch as he takes a seat on the lounger next to Harlyn who passes him the blunt. It's a heady sight watching him as he parts his perfect lips and wraps them around the end of the blunt. He takes a long pull and holds the smoke in for what seems like an eternity before slowly letting is waft out between slightly parted lips.

"You gotta little drool there, Nebraska," Harlyn whispers wiping at my mouth.

"Harlyn," I hiss, my cheeks heating.

She just laughs and falls back onto her lounger.

Zade looks at me through narrowed eyes as he passes the blunt back to Harlyn. "Nebraska?" he asks shifting his gaze to Harlyn. *Shit! He heard her.*

"Yeah, it's the new nickname I gave Fallon. Stray is old news. She's one of use now."

"Tell that to Bexley," he scoffs.

"Tell what to Bexley?" Alisander says as he steps out onto the terrace.

"I gave Fallon a new nickname," Harlyn says proudly.

"Oh really," Alisander says snatching the blunt from Harlyn and taking a long pull.

"Yep," Harlyn starts but Alisander holds up his hand.

"Doesn't matter what nickname you give her. Bex hates her and she'll always call her The Stray."

I love how they talk about me like I'm not here. "Or, everyone can just call me Fallon," I say looking from Alisander to Harlyn who both burst out laughing. Zade just stares out at the lake paying us no mind at all.

Alisander saunters over and plops down on the lounger on the other side of me.

"Only a few hours until sunrise," he says before lying back on the lounger and staring up at the night sky.

We all follow his lead, laying back, looking up at the stars, and not talking.

I don't know how long we sat out there under the night sky but after a good while Devya comes bursting through the terrace doors.

"I've been looking for you guys," she says.

I look over at her. Somethings changed. Her usual happy, care-free demeanor is gone. She looks agitated.

"Well you found us," Harlyn says, her attention still on the sky which is doing a slow crawl from darkness to light as the first rays of the sun casts away the cloak of night.

"Well, c'mon it's time," Devya says.

"Time for what?" I ask, craning my neck to look over at her.

She walks around and stands in front of us. "Time to meet in the media room. Time to see if everybody completed their task."

Harlyn lets out a long sigh then gets up. "Come on, Nebraska," she says looking over at me.

The serene calm of laying on the lounger watching the night sky fade to the dewy light of day turns to nerves and panic.

Yeah, I completed my task but this is all still so very new to me. I committed a crime only a few hours ago and now I'm about to be what? Judged and tried to see if I'm worthy of being in the inner circle. I swear this is something out of a movie.

I watch as Alisander and Zade both stand up, their faces stoic as they make their way into the house.

"Devya, are you alright?" I ask worried. She really doesn't seem like herself.

"I'm fine," she says then heads inside.

"Don't worry about Devya. She loses a little bit of her shine every year at this party. The things we have to do start to take a toll on some of us after a while," Harlyn says.

"What do you think she had to do?" I ask.

"Not sure. We've been attending these parties since freshman year and Devya's never once told me what her task was. I never know until we all meet in the media room. It's that we learn what everyone had to do."

"Well I'm worried about her."

"She'll be fine. Now, come on. Let's get this over with," Harlyn says grabbing my hand and pulling me up off the lounger.

CHAPTER FIFTEEN

The media room is this massive, contemporary space with a super-sized digital cinema screen, theater style seats, lots of custom cabinets and a whole snack counter complete with popcorn maker, candy, and soda machine.

All of the pure bloods are already inside when Harlyn and I walk in. The magnificent three are all seated at the back of the room. Bexley, Indigo, Tatum, and Chloe are seated together and three of the four Elmsley kids are all sitting in the same row. Me and Harlyn follow Devya into the front section and sit down.

I look around the room. My eyes fall on Bexley who scowls at me. I quickly turn around and face the front.

"Hey," I say leaning over to Harlyn. "One of the Elmsley boys is missing."

Harlyn does a quick survey of the room. "You're right. That's not a good sign."

"Why not?" I ask.

Before she can answer the lights dim and the screen flickers on.

A black silhouette of a man appears on the screen and a distorted voice floats through the sound system filling the room. "Hello, pure bloods. You were given a task to complete before sunrise. The sun has risen. Time to see which of you has what it takes to move within the ranks of the elite."

The screen goes black and it seems that all of the air leaves the room at the same time. It's so quiet and still that if an ant walked in and took a piss we'd hear it.

After a few seconds the same distorted voice floats through the sound system again. "Let's begin."

We all wait quietly as an image appears on the screen. It's Indigo and Tatum James.

"Indigo and Tatum James," the distorted voice says. "Step forward."

Indigo and Tatum walk to the front of the room. They're as confident as ever as they stand in front of the screen. Me, I'm a nervous wreck. I don't even realize I'm wringing my hands over an over until Harlyn reaches over and stills them by placing her hand over mine.

"Indigo and Tatum James, your task was to get compromising pictures of Headmaster Cromwell. Did you succeed or fail?"

A quiet beat passes before the word, success, appears on the screen in bold letters across their pictures.

Indigo and Tatum turn and face us, their identical faces both wearing an expression of complete unconcern as they make their way back to their seats.

The distorted voice sounds again, "Harlyn Ratcliffe and Chloe North," the voice says as their pictures appear on the screen.

Harlyn hops up and stands in front of the screen. Chloe takes her place beside her a few seconds later.

"Harlyn and Chloe, your task was to hack into the schools system and send all midterm exams to every pure blood. Did you succeed or fail?"

Just like with Indigo and Tatum, there is a moment of silence then the word success appears on the screen.

"As if I wouldn't succeed," Harlyn brags as she takes her seat next to me.

Chloe says nothing, she just walks quietly back to her seat and sits down.

Lucca's called next, then Alisander who both have the word success slapped across their pictures.

The Elmsley girls, Ariel Underwood and Becca Love are called to the front. "Ariel and Becca, your task was to vandalize the statue of Wilhelm Elmsley, the founder of Elmsley Academy. Did you succeed or fail?" Again, there's silence before the word success is stamped across their pictures.

"Zade Amherst, Bexley Barringer and Fallon Gamble," the distorted voice says.

I freeze at the sound of my name. I know that I completed my task and that I have nothing to worry about but a shiver of panic settles in my belly and I can't move.

"Go," Harlyn says jabbing elbowing me.

I shoot up out of my seat and stand next to Zade. There's no way I'm going to stand next to Bexley.

"Zade, Bexley and Fallon, your task was to set fire to Calais Vineyard. Did you succeed or fail?"

I don't realize I'm holding my breath until the word success appears on the screen and I let out a heavy sigh.

Bexley looks over at me, her pretty face set in a vicious expression. She looks as if wants to say something to me but she doesn't. Instead she does a snotty head-toss and goes back to her seat. Zade takes his seat next to Lucca and I sit back down next to Harlyn.

"Slade Waldgrave," the distorted voice says and the Elmsley boy makes his way to the front. "Slade, your task was to transfer funds from Bishop Winthrop's company account to a personal account in the Cayman Islands. Did you succeed or fail?"

Jeezus! He had to set someone up to look like they embezzled money. Who in the hell comes up with these tasks? It's crazy but I'm not surprised when the words success flashes across his picture.

"Devya Nadar," the voice calls out. Devya stands and moves stiffly to the front. "Devya Nadar, your task was to release the criminal record of Dex Michelson. Did you succeed for fail?"

Dex Michelson? Is he any relation to Cord Michelson? I look over at Harlyn whose brow is creased with worry and I get my answer. No wonder Devya's mood had gone sour. She was tasked with ruining the life of someone she really liked.

The word success appears across Devya's picture and I watch as she takes her seat. She looks numb and sad. I reach for her hand as she sits down but she folds it in her lap and stares straight ahead.

"Hunter Gryffon," the distorted voice says.

No one moves to the front of the room. The other Elmsley boy never showed up to the media room. His picture appears on the screen with the word Fail stamped across it.

"Hunter Gryffon failed to complete his task and like the coward he is, failed to show up and face his fate. Hunter Gryffon is a disgrace and is hereby shunned for a year. His family will be fined one hundred thousand dollars. This concludes the Dare Party. Remember, your family name is everything. Protect it at all costs," the distorted voice finishes then the screen goes black.

I turn to Harlyn. "How do they know who completed their task and who didn't?"

"Just know, someone's always watching," she says then stands up.

"That's not ominous or anything," I say.

Harlyn just laughs.

"So, now what?" I ask her.

"Now we head back to Bradford and don't ever speak about what happened here in this room," she says.

None of us speak as we make our way out of the media room and to the front of the mansion. There's a row of black SUVS with dark, tinted windows lining the driveway as we step outside. Zade, Alisander and Lucca get into the first car, Bexley, the twins and Chloe get into the second car, and me, Devya and Harlyn get into the third car. The Elmsley kids get into the last car then one by one the SUVs take off down the driveway and away from the mansion.

The drive back to Bradford is a quiet one. Me, Devya and Harlyn sit, each lost in our own thoughts. This night has to be the wildest, most surreal night of my life. I probably went through every possible emotion - fear, confusion, nerves, glee, longing, passion. Just to name a few. I'm utterly exhausted. I have no idea how these kids have gone through this night several times already. I'd be bat-shit crazy by now if I were them.

I steal a glance at Devya. Her eyes are closed and her head is pressed firmly into the headrest of her seat. I'm worried about her. I lean forward and reach my hand out to tap her shoulder but Harlyn stops me.

"Don't," she mouths.

"But I'm worried about her," I whisper.

"Give her some time. She'll talk to us when she's ready."

I nod, sit back in my seat and stare out the window into the passing darkness as the SUV speeds quietly across the empty highway back to Bradford.

The car comes to a quiet stop in front of Amherst Hall just as the sun has finished its descent into the sky welcoming daylight as if it has no idea of the dirty deeds we did last night.

I look at the clock on my cell phone. It's 7 a.m.

"Will you guys stay over at my place?" Devya asks.

"Of course," I say without a thought. Devya still looks devastated. I'm sure she needs moral support which I'm more than happy to give. She's been a good friend to me since I arrived at Bradford. The least I can do is be there for her when she needs me.

"Sure thing," Harlyn chimes in before climbing out of the car.

We're silent as we walk into the building and make our way to Devya's room. We say nothing as she tosses oversized t-shirts to me and Harlyn to wear to bed. We all climb into Devya's bed and with her sandwiched between us, we quickly fall asleep.

I wish I could say I got the peaceful sleep I needed but of course that's not what happened. As soon as I close my eyes I'm plagued with dreams of fire, lust and pain. My dream starts out amazing. I'm running through a vineyard and Zade is playfully chasing me. He catches me and we tumble playfully to the ground where he kisses me senseless. His body is hard against my soft flesh and his kisses are fire against my willing lips. We're completely lost in each other when out of nowhere Bexley shows up. Next thing I know she's dragging me by the hair through the vineyard. She stops in the middle of a large group of vines and douses me and the vines with gasoline before pulling out a lighter and igniting the flame. I beg her not to set me ablaze but she just laughs and drops the lighter on me and I immediately go up in flames.

The sound of a cell phone ringing jolts me out of my sleep and I'm thankful to be pulled out of the nightmare.

"Hello Pita," Devya says into her cell phone. She listens for a few seconds then, "Yes, I know." She climbs out of bed and paces back and forth across the room.

I pretend to be asleep as I listen to her talk.

"It was as hard this year as it was last year. It just doesn't get any easier," she says then pauses. "Mujhe pata hai, Pita. Family first." Another pause. "Okay. I should go. Harlyn and Fallon are here." Another pause. "Yes, I love you too. Bye Pita," Devya says and hangs up the phone. "I know you're awake," she says moving back over to the bed.

I roll over and look up at her. "Sorry. I wasn't eavesdropping. I promise. I just didn't want to disturb you," I say sitting up.

"It's fine. We should get up anyway. We can go into town and have a late lunch," she says getting out of bed.

"What time is it?" I ask.

"A little after one," she replies.

"Okay," I say then look over at Harlyn whose still sound asleep and snoring. "What about this one?"

Devya's face splits into a wide grin. "Snorey-snorerton? Wake her up," Devya giggles.

"Harlyn!" I yell and give her a good nudge.

She shoots straight up in bed. "What the hell you ass," she frowns, taking a pillow and chucking it at me.

"Time to get up," Devya says. "We're going out for a late lunch."

Harlyn rolls her eyes and falls back onto the pile of pillows.

We shower at Devya's and borrow clothes to wear to lunch. We take Harlyn's Porsche to a cute little French inspired cafe called Soul Kitchen about thirty minutes from the school. It's a very rustic joint with shabby chic vibes and they offer a menu of fresh, organic foods for really reasonable prices. We find a table near the back of the restaurant and a waitress comes over immediately to greet us.

"Welcome to Soul Kitchen. Here's your menus. Can I get you anything to drink?" she asks.

"I'll take a double shot espresso," Harlyn says.

"I'll have a café crème," Devya says.

"I'm not much of a coffee drinker so I guess just give me a green tea," I say.

"Very good. I'll be right back with your drinks," the waitress says and leaves.

"How do you not drink coffee, Fallon?" Harlyn frowns. "I can't make it through the day without my morning cup of joe."

"I don't know. I guess it's because my mom wasn't a coffee drinker. We drank a lot of tea in my house," I say.

"I guess," Harlyn says then looks over at Devya who's staring quietly out the window. "You good?" she asks her.

"I don't know. This year's dare was probably the worse one for me. It's personal, you know? It's going to affect someone I really care about."

"Yeah, you and Cord were really starting to get close," Harlyn says.

"As soon as the media circuit picks up the story about his father, things are going to get bad for him and his family and it going to be my fault," she says, a pained look on her face.

"He won't know it's your fault unless you tell him." Harlyn says.

"True but I'll know. And what happens if this thing between us gets serious? He'll hate me if he ever finds out that I was the cause of his father's ruin."

"Maybe it won't be such a big deal in the news," I offer.

"Oh, it'll be a big deal. It's Dare Party business which means it was done for a reason and will have major impact," Harlyn explains.

The waitress returns with our drinks, takes our order and disappears again.

I look at Devya who looks sad and utterly defeated. I reach out and squeeze her shoulder. "I'm sorry Devya. I wish there was something I could do."

"It's okay, Fallon. I'll be fine. You'd think I would be used to all the craziness that comes with this life."

"I'm not sure how anyone could ever get used to this. I know I won't," I say.

"I just try not to let it bother me," Harlyn says. "It's not like I can ever get out of it. Unless I want to end up dead broke and outcast."

"Let's not talk about it anymore. It's too depressing." Devya says.

"Winter breaks coming up. And you know what that means," Harlyn says, a big smile gracing her lips.

"Aspen!" Devya blurts out, her eyes lighting up.

"Aspen," Harlyn says with a wicked grin.

"I mentioned it to Fallon last night but didn't go into the details," Devya says.

"Yeah, you told me that all the pure bloods go over winter break."

"Yep, it's hella crazy. There's skiing and snowboarding, and Alisander throws this crazy ass party every year. It's so much fun," Harlyn says wiging her eyebrows.

"You're coming right, Fallon?" Devya asks, her eyes pleading.

don't know. I'd have to check with my grandfather. I think…"

"He'll be fine with you going. Trust me," Harlyn says.

"Why do you say that?"

"Because all the pure bloods will be there which means that you need to be there too so you're clued in on everything. You don't want Bexley out there campaigning for your demise and you not being there to shoot her down, do you?"

"Planning my demise? I thought I'm in the clear now that I survived the Dare Party," I say, a sense of dread bubbling up in my stomach.

"Bexley hates you. You'll never be in the clear," Devya says.

CHAPTER SIXTEEN

Monday morning rolls around and I'm sitting in my early morning therapy session with Mr. Blackmore. Not much has changed since our first session. I sit quietly while he asks me questions.

"Did you have a good weekend, Fallon?" Mr. Blackmore asks.

Let's see, I attended a secret dinner party for Texas' elite, drank, had some weed candy and, oh, I burned down a vineyard. "It was okay," I say.

"Just okay?" He asks, tapping his pen against his knee.

"I had brunch with two friends yesterday." I have to give him something.

"That's good. So, you've made another friend, then?"

"Yeah, I guess," I say not bothering to elaborate.

He writes something down in his notepad then looks over at me. I guess he's waiting for me to say something else. And believe me there's so much I could say but why bother. And why drag him into all this inner circle, elite bullshit. So, I stay tight-lipped.

"How are your tutoring sessions going with Lucca?" He asks.

"Fine."

"So, you two are getting along?"

If you call making out every day against the door to the faculty library getting along, then I say yes. "Yep," I say.

He nods and jots down more notes. "And what about your mom? Any new issues come up around that?"

My entire body stiffens at the mention of my mom. I've been so distracted with all the pure blood nonsense that my mom hasn't been in my thoughts as much as she should be. A rush of guilt washes over me. She should be the foremost thing on my mind but here I am running around with these entitled brats who think fucking up someone's world in the name of family is okay. My stomach twists and catapults bile into my throat and I struggle not to throw up. I'm disgusted with myself. How can I just forget about my mom?

"Fallon," Mr. Blackmore calls but I barely register his voice.

I can feel the tears coming on, pricking at the corners of my eyes just waiting to spill over.

"Fallon, it's okay to cry. You lost someone very important to you," Mr. Blackmore says, his voice soothing.

I'm sure he's right but crying at Bradford is just weakness, no matter the reason. So, I shove it down. The pain, the loss, the image of my mother dying in that hospital bed. I shove it all down. When I look back at Mr. Blackmore my face is an uninterested mask again.

He watches me closely for a few moments then jots more notes in his notepad.

He doesn't ask me anymore questions. We just sit quietly for the remainder of the session which is fine with me.

Chemistry class is a blur. Zade's not in class and Chloe and the twins pay me no mind. I assume it's because I survived the Dare Party and they have to leave me alone.

Devya meets me after class and we walk to English class together. She's a total chatterbox and is going on about the winter break trip to Aspen. She's pretty much planned the whole trip already. I think focusing on that keeps her mind off what she did to Cord's father. That little stunt of hers hasn't had any impact yet but Harlyn's pretty adamant that it will eventually.

My mind's still on mom. I really miss her. I'm pretty sure she's looking down from heaven at me in disappointment. The things I've done since I've been at Bradford are not indicative of how she raised me. I mean I set fire to a vineyard for God's sake.

"Fallon, are you listening to me?" Devya says. She's stopped walking and is standing a few paces behind me.

"Sorry, what?" I say.

"Forget it. We'll talk about it later. Let's just get to class," she says and moves past me down the hall.

By the time lunch rolls around I'm ready for the day to be over so I can retreat to my room. Lasagna which is one of my favorite meals, is on the menu today. I order it but just pick at it at instead of eating it.

"Fallon, are you okay? You've been distant all morning." Devya says.

"I'm fine," I sigh. "I've just been missing my mom today is all."

"I'm sorry," she says, looking at me with careful sympathy.

"It's fine. I really need to snap out of it anyway."

My cell phone dings. It's Harlyn saying to meet her in the courtyard now. The word now is in all caps followed by three exclamation points.

look at Devya. "Harlyn wants us to meet her in the courtyard."

"Now?" Devya asks.

I hold up my phone and show her the message and her eyes bug out.

"Let's go," she says grabbing my hand and pulling me along behind her.

The courtyard's empty except for a couple of students sitting around reading. Harlyn's sitting on the arm of one of the outdoor sofas. She jumps up and waves us over as soon as we step outside. We make our way over to her and as we get closer I can see panic in her eyes.

"What's going on?" I ask.

She grabs me and Devya by the arm and pulls us close. "Have you gotten any news alerts?" She asks.

"What? No. Why?" I ask.

She holds up her phone and there on the screen is the news headline, *Son of Calais Vineyard owner dies in fire.*

My mouth goes dry and my vision immediately blurs. My

heart takes off and thunders against my chest. This can't be happening. Me, Zade and Bexley set fire to that vineyard. If someone's dead that means that we killed him. I feel lightheaded and nauseous. Suddenly everything's blurry and then total blackness.

"Put this on her forehead."

"Are you sure we shouldn't take her to the nurse?"

"I caught her before she hit the ground so she's not hurt. We just need to wake her up."

I can hear Devya and Harlyn talking about me but I can't see them. In fact, all I see is blackness.

"Fallon," Harlyn says. "Wake up."

"Open your eyes, Fallon." That's Devya talking now. "Maybe we should slap her. That always works in the movies," she says.

"Fallon, wake up," Harlyn says slapping me lightly on the cheek.

"She's not waking up," Devya says, her voice panicked. "Maybe we should call someone."

"We're not calling anyone," Harlyn snaps.

"Maybe slap her harder then," Devya suggests, her voice laced with panic.

"Just give her a minute. Fallon!" Harlyn says my name with force and slaps my cheek a little harder.

My eyes fly open.

"Well, that did it," Harlyn says sounding relieved.

"What happened?" I ask looking from Harlyn to Devya.

"You fainted," Devya says.

"I fainted?"

"Yes," Harlyn says, looking half concerned and half annoyed.

I'm still feeling a bit dizzy but I sit up. "Why would I faint?"

Devya and Harlyn exchange looks.

"Let's go to your dorm," Devya says. "We can talk about it there."

"We have class," I protest.

"Screw class. This is more important," Harlyn says helping me up.

We hurry to Barringer Hall and Devya locks the door after we get inside my room.

"Sit down," she orders as she turns to face me

She looks tense and nervous so I do as she says.

"And don't faint again," she says.

"I'll do my best," I frown.

"Do you remember what we were talking about before you fainted?" She asks.

"Harlyn was telling us something about Calais Vineyards."

Devya looks at Harlyn. "I'm just going to say it. If she faints again at least were inside and out of public view."

"Say what?" I ask confused.

"Frances Calais, the son of the owner of Calais Vineyards died."

"Okay..."

"At the vineyard...Saturday night...in the fire," Harlyn says watching me closely.

"Oh, fuck!" I say, panic and fear wrapping around me like a vice grip.

"Okay, Fallon, you have to breathe," Devya says, her voice soothing.

"Fuck! Fuck! Fuck! We killed him. I killed him. What are we going to do? We have to go to the police," I ramble.

"No, no, no, no, no," Harlyn says coming over and bracing her hands on my shoulders. "You can't go to the police."

"But we killed someone," I shout as tears sting the back of my eyes.

"Fallon, you'll go to jail. And so will Zade and Bexley. Listen to me, just calm down and we'll figure this out," she says looking me in the eyes.

"I can't be calm, Harlyn a man is dead!"

"A boy...a boy is dead," Devya whispers.

"What?" I say whipping around to look at her.

"Frances Calais was seventeen. He went to school here."

My body goes limp at her words and Harlyn has to hold me up. I killed a boy. A teenager like me. I'm a murderer. I'm a horrible person and I deserve whatever comes my way.

"We have to call the police. We have to tell them what we did," I whisper then jerk out of Harlyn's grip.

I make a beeline for my cell phone on the counter but Devya grabs it before I can get to it.

"Give me my phone!" I shout.

"No! Fallon, you're not thinking straight. You can't call the police. Just let us help you. We'll figure out what to do together."

"What's there to figure out? I killed someone and I should be punished."

"You didn't know he was in the vineyard. It's not your fault," Devya reasons.

"Are you kidding me?" I scoff. "I helped douse those vines with gasoline. I stood by and watched while Zade lit the match. It is my fault. Now give me my damn phone!" I lunge at Devya but she side-steps me and runs into the bathroom and locks the door.

"Fallon, please. You have to calm down. I know this is a crazy situation but we need to be rational here. Let's just talk about our options and if you still want to go to the police after then fine."

My heart is racing and I'm terrified. I don't even realize that I've started pacing back and forth across the room. "Options? What options? Harlyn, a boy is dead because of me. There's only one option."

Suddenly there's a loud knock on the door and my heart bottoms out. I just know it's the police. Harlyn and I share a panicked look.

Devya comes racing out of the bathroom and yanks open the door. I'm shocked to see Zade standing on the other side, his raven colored hair pushed back off his beautiful, hard-edged face. His lips are pressed in a firm, angry line and those blue-violet eyes pierce right through me. He strides through the door and walks right up to me.

"You cool?" He asks, his velvety penetrating the wall of panic that seems to have resurrected itself around me.

"No," I say shaking my head. My entire world is crumbling

around me. This has really been a shit year. Starting with the death of my mom, then the move to Texas into a home with a grandfather who's basically a stranger, followed by me being shipped off to Bradford with a bunch of rich, asshole kids who did nothing but bully me. And now I'm a murderer. How can I be cool?

"She keeps threatening to go the police," Devya says.

I look over at her. She's got a death grip on my phone and she's biting down so hard on her bottom lip it's no wonder that she doesn't draw blood.

Zade locks those beautiful eyes with mine and I'm stuck. I couldn't move if I wanted to.

"You can't go to the police, Fallon. Doing that will blow up your entire life," he says, his voice calm, soothing.

"My life has already blown up. A boy is dead, Zade. We killed him," I say through clenched teeth.

"We didn't know anyone would be in the vineyard that late at night. It was an accident."

"It doesn't matter and it doesn't change what we did. I'm not this person who hurts people and just walks away. My mom didn't raise me like that. I'm not like you guys." My voice is getting louder, stronger. I back away from Zade. "You all hurt people and you don't care. It's not right." I say and make a bee-line for the door. I have to get out of there.

Zade and Harlyn are on my heels as I snatch open the door and race down the hall. I can hear Harlyn and Devya calling my name but I don't stop running. I pass the elevator and make my way to the stairs. As I turn the corner I run smack dab into Bexley. Indigo is with her.

"Watch it, Stray," she bits out and pushes me to the ground.

I'm really not in the mood for her shit right now. I jump up and shove her hard. She stumbles back, her eyes rounding in shock.

"You bitch," she screams and lunges at me.

"Fuck you," I shout as we crash into each other, grabbing each other around the neck and tussling.

"A boy died in that fire we started at the vineyard and I'm going to the police and tell them what we did," I say through gritted teeth.

"Like hell you are," Bexley says and slaps me so hard my head spins. "I'll kill you before I let you do that," she says and lunges at me a second time.

"Zade, stop her!" Devya yells.

Zade throws himself between us. He pushes Bexley back and grabs me around the waist. "Get her out of here, Indigo. I'll take care of Fallon."

Indigo nods and tries to pull Bexley in the other direction but the girl is seething mad. She's not going anywhere if it's not in the direction where I'm at.

"Harlyn, help her," Zade says as he pulls me down the hall.

"Let me go!" I scream as I wiggle, push and flail my arms trying to get out of Zade's grip.

Zade wraps me in a bear hug pressing my body firmly against his. His black licorice and cola scent surrounds me. His smell combined with the feel of body on mine is so comforting that I can't help but calm down a bit.

He grabs my chin forcing me to look at him. His face is so close to mine that I can feel his breath, mint with a hint of tobacco, fan across my lips. "Fallon, listen to me. Let me get you out of here. I know someplace we can go. Just you and me. You can calm down and we can talk about this, okay?"

I'm still very worked up. My chest is heaving and I'm breathing like a madwoman. But his presence is calming. I start to relax a little.

Zade cradles the side of my face and stares straight into my eyes. "Please just come with me, Fallon."

Quiet, brooding Zade Amherst is pleading with me to go with him. This is something that I never would have imagined. And it's probably something that would never happen if it weren't for the current situation but it is happening and I can't resist the look of desperation in those blue-violet eyes.

I stop fighting him. "Fine," I whisper and without another word I allow him to whisk me out of there.

He leads me to the parking lot and over to his motorcycle. I stand stiff and numb as he places a helmet on my head then lifts me onto the bike before climbing on himself.

"Hold on tight," he says as I wrap my arms around his waist. He revs up the bike and speeds off.

He drives for a long time, racing down the highway then turning off onto a long county road lined with nothing but grass fields and trees. We speed down the county road for miles before he turns onto a side road that itself goes on for miles. There's nothing but trees and grass all around for miles then to my left a beautiful lake comes into view. I can see cabins scattered around the lake.

Zade turns the bike onto a long driveway leading to a beautiful log cabin sitting on posts elevating it high off the ground. The cabin is right off the lake and has an amazing wooded walkway leading from the cabin and jutting out over the water.

We come to a stop and Zade hops off the bike then helps me off. He pulls the helmet off of me and hangs it on the handlebars. He doesn't say anything. He just makes his way over to the cabin, unlocks the door and goes inside. I follow quietly behind him.

The inside of the cabin is just as beautiful as the outside. The entrance leads straight into a great room with large windows overlooking the lake. There's a fireplace, a large flat screen television and big, comfy oversized furniture.

Zade stands in the middle of all of the splendor carefully watching me. "This is the living room," he says cutting through the silence. "The kitchen's over there," he says pointing to his left. "There's a bathroom over there and the bedrooms are down the hall."

This place is beautiful and under any other circumstance I would be running through the house exploring the many rooms but these aren't normal circumstances. In fact, nothing in my life is normal right now. I don't even know who I am anymore and I doubt any of my old friends would even recognize me. What I did, helping set that vineyard on fire is terrible. And the worst part is that it was my choice. Zade didn't force me and as much as I hate Bexley she didn't force me either. The choice was mine and I chose wrong and now a boy is dead. I have no idea how I'm going to live with myself.

CHAPTER SEVENTEEN

"Do you want something to drink?" Zade asks moving towards the kitchen.

"Sure," I whisper just barely finding my voice.

I watch as he goes into the kitchen, which is all beautifully glossed stained wood with open facing cabinets and stainless steel appliances. Zade grabs two glasses off the shelf then opens a cabinet and pulls out a bottle of bourbon. He fills both glasses halfway then walks back over and hands one to me.

I take a big gulp expecting the brown liquid to be nasty and burn on the way down. Surprisingly the notes of vanilla, oak and caramel are smooth, almost pleasant. I put the glass back up to my lips and finish it.

Zade is watching me through hooded eyes as he walks over and takes the glass out of my hand and sits it on the coffee table.

"Guess you needed that," he says.

"I guess so."

He sits down in the armchair across from the sofa. Keeping his eyes on me, he brings his glass to his lips and takes a sip. I can almost imagine the way his mouth feels watching him slip the glass between his lips. And the way he's watching me while he does it - I feel completely exposed.

I don't know what to do with myself so I sit down on the sofa.

We sit in silence for a while just looking at each other. All kinds of thoughts are running through my head. Thoughts of the fire, thoughts about the dead Calais boy, thoughts about my mother. And in between all of those thoughts are images of Zade and his beautiful eyes. Eyes that watch me now. I fidget on the couch, placing my hands in my lap then folding them across my chest, then putting them back in my lap. He's never looked at me this long and it's making me nervous. Not to mention the silence. It's killing me. I have to say something.

"What is this place?" I ask him.

"It's a cabin," he says then takes a sip of his drink.

"Clearly," I snap, rolling my eyes.

He takes another sip of his bourbon then rests the glass on his knee. "It was my grandfather's cabin. He left it to me when he died."

"Oh," I say, remembering what Devya told me about him being close to his grandfather. "Do you come here often?"

"I spend a good amount of time here," he shrugs.

"Well it's a beautiful cabin," I say.

"Thank you."

We go quiet again. The only sounds are the soft song of birds flying around outside.

"Zade, why did you bring me here?" I ask.

He shrugs. "Devya called. She said you were freaking out about Frances Calais dying in the fire and that you were threatening to go to the police. I came to see if I could talk you off the ledge but you were already too far gone when I got there. And you and Bex, well, ya'll would have torn each other apart so I figured I'd better get you out of there."

"But why did you bring me here?" I ask again.

"Because no one knows about this place."

"But you said you spend a good amount of time here."

"Yeah, I come here. Alone. To get away," he says then takes another sip of his drink.

"So, you've never brought anyone else here?" I ask.

"Nope."

I get that he was trying to remove me from a volatile situation but why bring me here to his private getaway? It may sound crazy given the circumstances but I feel sort of special. I'm the first person he's ever brought here.

Zade gets up and grabs my glass off the coffee table. "Want a refill?"

"Sure." I watch him as he walks back to the kitchen, shoulders swaying, arms swinging just a bit, and nice even relaxed stride. I shake my head. The boy is pure swag. I pull my bottom lip between my teeth and bite down to try and get myself together. I cannot let Zade's sexy ass distract me from what's going on. I'm still the cause of a boy's death after all.

Zade comes back from the kitchen and hands me my glass then sits right in front of me on the coffee table. He looks at me for a few moments, his eyes studying my face before he leans in closer. I don't mean to but I inhale deeply taking in his delicious scent.

"So, I guess we should talk about what happened," he says.

"You mean about how we started a fire and killed someone," I say, not sugar coating it.

He flinches for a second then his face goes neutral. "I wouldn't put it that way but sure."

"What is there to talk about? We caused that boy's death, Zade."

"Maybe. I guess," he says.

"What do you mean maybe? There is no maybe. We started the fire, Zade."

"I know that, Fallon," he says scrubbing his hand down his face. "Yes, we started the fire but we didn't know anyone was in that vineyard. We didn't go there to kill anyone."

"But we did, Zade. We did!"

His eyes close and he lets out a heavy sigh. When he opens them again the violet color that sits in their depths is gone. They've intensified and darkened to a deep blue.

"And you think going to the police and confessing is the answer," he says more than asks.

"I think that we ended someone's life and that we should face the consequences of that," I say.

"So, you're fine with spending the rest of your life in jail?"

I start to speak, to tell him yes but that would be a lie. I don't want to spend the rest of my life in jail. I want to finish high school. I want to go to college. I want to live the life that my mom wanted for me.

"Yeah, I didn't think so," he says sitting up straight. "Going to the police is exactly what that will get you, Fallon. Life in jail."

I drop my head and stare down at my hands. I know what we did was wrong. I know that we should pay for it but he's right, I don't want to spend the rest of my life in jail.

"And you know what else?" He says putting his finger under my chin and tipping my head up. "Bexley's not going to own up to anything. There's no proof that she was there. Hell, there's no proof that I was there. You'd be confessing all alone."

"You'd let me take the fall by myself?" I ask, a sinking feeling in the pit of my stomach.

"It's not what I'd want to do. But it's what I'd have to do, Fallon."

The sinking feeling in my stomach becomes an abyss. I really want him to be on my side. "Why would you have to, Zade?" I ask, already knowing the answer.

"Because it's what would be good for my family. I'm the sole heir to the Amherst empire. I can't confess to murder. I can't go to jail," he says looking at me like I should know all this already.

"Family over everything," I say between clenched teeth.

"Exactly."

As much as I like Zade invading my space I can't be this close to him right now. I get up and go stand by the window and stare out at the lake. I don't hear him move but I know he's standing behind me. I can feel his heat. Smell his scent.

"Fallon," he says placing his hand on my shoulder. "I know this is difficult for someone like you to understand but it's the way it is with people like us who come from powerful families."

I turn on him. "So what? You just kill people and go about your life like nothing happened?"

He just looks at me. His silence telling me what I already know.

"It's not right and you know it."

"I didn't say it was right, Fallon. It's just the way it is."

"But it shouldn't be this way. You can't just kill someone and act like it didn't happen."

"Who's acting like it didn't happen? I found out about it around the same time you did then Devya called. I didn't even have time to really process it."

"That may be true but you don't care to process it. Look at you. You're completely fine and I'm a mess. I'm completely broken by this. I don't even think I'll be able to look at myself in the mirror again. I'm not a good person. I used to be. But not anymore. Not after this." The tears come crashing down like a tidal wave and there's nothing I can do to stop them.

Zade grabs me and wraps me in his arms. He holds me tightly to him and I cry. I cry for my mother who died too soon. I cry for a boy who died because I was too much of a coward to do the right thing. I cry because no matter how much I want to, I know I'm not going to the police. I cry the most because the innocent girl from the Midwest is gone and I'm not sure if I'll ever get her back.

I look up at Zade, fat tears fall in droves down my cheeks. "Zade, I..."

"Shhh," he says running his thumb across my cheek wiping away the tears. "You don't have to say anything. I know."

I search his eyes. The soft violet color has returned and I'm lost in their blue-violet depths. Neither one of us speak. Everything is quiet. The only sound is the mingling of our breaths.

The air around us thickens and sizzles. Zade curls his fingers around the back of my head and pulls me close, hovering his warm lips above mine. He pauses there for what feels like forever, making me realize how much I want him to kiss me, how much I need him to kiss me. How much I want to get lost in his kiss and for it to taste like oblivion, for it to take me under and drown my pain.

Zade slants his mouth over mine and his hot tongue slides between my lips, taking complete control over me, over the situation. I melt into him and allow myself to drown in the sweetness of his tongue.

His kiss is like no other kiss I've had before. It's nothing like the clumsy first kiss I had with my seventh grade crush. It's not like the gentle but urgent kisses that I shared with Lucca or the sweet, gentle kiss I shared with Alisander, no, Zade kisses with all the experience of a grown man, like someone who knows his way around a woman's body.

I moan against his lips and curl my fingers in the soft hairs at the base of his neck.

When he pushes me back against the window, I welcome it, loving the feel of the cold glass against my back, loving how he slides his hand over the curve of my hip sending hot thrills of fire through me. My body feels achy and my thighs clench tight as I run my hands down his chest and under his t-shirt. I trail my fingers along the hard ridges of his abdomen. His body is so sculpted and muscular. I've never gone this far with a boy before, having his naked skin beneath my fingertips. I'm excited. I want more.

I press my pelvis against his as I run my hands up his chest and trace my fingers over his nipple.

Zade grunts and grabs hold of my hair - hard, making my scalp sting a little as he fists tawny strands around his knuckles and yanks. His tongue is urgent as it drives between my lips, claiming every last part of me. I'm so caught up that I barely notice when his hand drops down and slips inside the waistband of my Bradford uniform skirt. His fingers slide down the front of my panties and between my thighs. The fabric is wet. I know it and now so does he. He runs his fingers back and forth causing the most delicious friction, causing me to get wetter. He moves my panties aside and runs a finger up my wet slit and I freeze. I freeze because no one's ever touched me like that. It's such a new sensation. I like it, I'm just not sure what to do.

Zade stills his hand. He pulls back from the kiss and rests his forehead against mine. His breathing is heavy - deep. His eyes lock on mine. "You're a virgin," he says, his tone accusing.

I nod because I can't find my voice to speak.

He closes his eyes and lets out a long, slow breath as if he's trying to get ahold of himself. He pulls his hand from inside my skirt and brings his fingers to his mouth and sucks the wetness from them.

"We should stop," he says. "You're not in the right headspace right now."

"No, I'm...I'm fine."

"A lot has happened, Fallon. You're upset. People do things they wouldn't normally do when they're upset." He steps back a little putting some space between us.

"Maybe, but that's not what I'm doing. I want this...I want you." And I mean that. I never wanted anything more than to be with Zade right now. To lose myself in him.

He runs his thumb across my bottom lip. "I'm sorry but I can't."

"Zade, please," I beg, fisting his t-shirt and pulling him back to me.

His nostrils flare and his eyes blaze cobalt as he crashes his mouth onto mine. His kiss is hard, punishing. He rakes his fingers in the hairs at the nape of my neck and tugs. My head falls back and he attacks my neck licking and sucking the sensitive skin there.

I'm dizzy with passion and drunk with need. I try to move my head to bring my mouth back to his but he tightens his grip on my hair holding my head in place. He runs his mouth along my chin and up to my ear.

"This isn't happening, Fallon. Not like this. When I fuck you for the first time it won't be because you're upset and you want to drown out the pain. It'll be when your mind is free of distraction. It will be when you're so turned on that your legs will part for me with one look and I'll happily bury myself deep between your thighs." And with that he releases my hair from his grip then turns and walks out the front door.

I'm left standing there, back against the window, chest heaving, completely aroused and utterly confused.

CHAPTER EIGHTEEN

A good several minutes pass before I move from the spot Zade left me. I'm completely shook by what just happened. I've been wanting Zade Amherst since I stepped on his shoe that first day of orientation. There's just something about him. The brooding, the quiet danger, the beautiful eyes.

I close my eyes and run my fingertips across my lips, reliving the feeling of his mouth on mine, the sweet taste of bourbon on his tongue. The way he dug his fingers into my scalp. The masterful way he commanded my mouth and my body. With him, in that moment, I was able to forget everything that happened. He did that. Being with him did that.

I let out a frustrated sigh and push off the window. I offered myself up to him and he literally ran away. Is it too much for me to have just one thing go my way?

I walk over to the front door and look out, hoping to see Zade sitting on the porch or standing in the grass by the lake but he's not in either of those places. I push open the screen door, step outside and look around the property. He's nowhere in sight. I notice his motorcycle is no longer where he parked it.

"Son of a bitch! Did he really leave me here?" I ask to no one in particular seeing how I'm the only one out here.

I walk around to the back of the house to see if he's there. He's not. In fact, the only thing back there is a lone hammock hanging between two trees.

How could he just leave me here? In the middle of nowhere especially after kissing me senseless and touching me the way no other guy ever has. And to make things worse, he seemed angry when he left. Now I'm stuck in the middle of God knows where with no cell phone and no idea when he's coming back.

I march back into the house, grab my glass off the table and fill it with bourbon. If I'm going to be stuck here in this cabin alone for who knows how long, I might as well get drunk.

I have no idea what time it is when I wake up. I just know my head is pounding like a thunderous bass drum. I look over at the almost empty bottle of bourbon sitting on the coffee table and groan. I almost finished the entire bottle which is crazy because I don't really drink all that much. Fooling with Zade's got me doing things I don't normally do. For instance, making out against a window and unashamedly telling a guy how much I want them. I close my eyes against the memory.

I have no idea how long I was passed out but what I do know is that my mouth is dry and my breath reeks like hell. I sit up and the pounding in my head gets a little bit louder. I head to the bathroom in search of some mouthwash and aspirin.

I find mouthwash, toothpaste and a new toothbrush in the bathroom of one of the bedrooms. I quickly brush my teeth, ridding my mouth of the stale, rank smell from my bourbon binge. I grab the washcloth hanging on the rack near the sink and wash my face. My hairs a little messy but I don't bother to do anything with it.

The house is quiet as I make my way out of the bedroom. Zade still hasn't returned and the sun that was shining brightly through the windows earlier is dimming as day settles into evening.

I go back into the living room and plop down on the couch. I'm stuck in this cabin all by myself, no cell phone and nothing to do. I look over at the large flat screen. I could watch television but I never really watched it at home so that's a no. I sigh and sink down onto the couch. I feel like I'll lose my mind just sitting so I get up and make my way down the hallway, deciding to explore the house. Zade gave me the minimalist tour when we arrived so I'll just check the place out myself. If there's anything here he doesn't want me to see, too bad. He shouldn't have left me here alone.

I bypass the first bedroom. I already saw it. It's the room I went into to use the bathroom. I open the door to it and peek inside. It's a fairly large room with a decent size bed and your standard bedroom furniture - dresser, nightstand, and small television. I move to the room across the hall. It must be the master bedroom. It's much larger than the other two rooms and there's a massive California King bed against the far wall outfitted with a thick, white comforter and a plethora of pillows. There's a large flat screen television on one wall and some really amazing artwork gracing the other walls in the room. I study them. They're really beautiful and have a surrealist quality to them. There's one painting in particular that catches my eye. It's a drawing of a faceless man whose body is made up of windows - some open, some closed. It reminds me a bit of Salvador Dali's *City of Drawers* drawing. The initials Z.A. grace the bottom of the picture. As I move around the room looking at all the paintings, I notice the initials Z.A at the bottom of them all and start to wonder if these were all done by Zade. If they are, he's more talented than I thought.

I leave the master bedroom and make my way to the last room at the end of the hallway. I'm in awe as I step through the door. It's not a bedroom at all. It's an art studio and it's amazing. There's a large rectangular craft table in the center of the room covered with all sorts of art supplies. A large easel sits in the corner by a set of floor to ceiling windows that overlook the lake. I bet the lighting during the day is perfect for painting. A canvas with the beginning stages of a painting sits on the easel and there's a stack of canvases sitting against the wall. I kneel down and look through them. It's a bunch of completed paintings. Each one in that similar surrealist style like the paintings in the master bedroom, each one breathtakingly beautiful.

"What are you doing in here?"

I jump as the sound of Zade's deep, raspy voice cuts through the silence. I turn to see him leaning against the doorframe. "You left me here alone. I was bored."

"So, you decided to snoop," he says, folding his arms across his chests.

"These are amazing," I say, ignoring his accusation and pointing to the canvases sitting against the wall. "Did you do them?"

Zade looks me up and down, his raven hair falling across his forehead, a hint of remembered passion peeking out of those beautiful blue-violet eyes. He pushes off the wall and strolls towards me. He looks at me with fire rearing in his eyes, darkening his blue-violet gaze to black. I can almost see his pulse thundering in his throat and I swear I can hear his heart beating. He stops right in front of me and runs his tongue across his lower lip and rakes his fingers through his hair.

Now I can hear my heart beating. He's so damn sexy. I want to reach out and touch him but I'm afraid he'll run out and leave me again.

His eyes travel to my lips and I get the feeling he wants to kiss me. But he doesn't. Instead he moves past me and bends down in front of the canvases.

"Yeah, these are mine," he says.

I kneel down next to him. "You're an amazing artist, Zade. Much better than I am."

"Thanks, but don't be so hard on yourself. I saw your work in art class. You're really good, Fallon."

My cheeks heat at his compliment. "Thanks."

"C'mon," he says standing up and moving towards the door.

I follow behind him. "Are we going back to Bradford now?"

"Nah, we're gonna stay here tonight," he says continuing down the hall and into the living room.

"We can't stay here. I don't have any clothes and we have school tomorrow."

"I brought you a change of clothes and some toiletries," he says, pointing to a Gucci duffle bag on the floor next to the front door.

"You brought me clothes," I say, going over to the duffle bag and bending down. Inside is one of my nightshirts, some underwear, a pair of jeans, a t-shirt and a pair of tennis shoes. I look over at him. "You went into my dorm room?"

"Nah, Devya did. She packed that bag for you." He disappears into the kitchen and returns with a bag full of Chinese food, two plates and a couple sodas. He sits everything on the coffee table. "I got dinner."

My stomach grumbles at the word dinner. I hadn't even realized that I hadn't eaten all day. I walk over and sit down on the floor next to the coffee table and watch as Zade pulls several containers out of a bag.

"We got shrimp fried rice, spring rolls, chow mein, Mongolian beef, some crab puffs and some stir fried veggies," he says, opening each container. He passes me a pair of chopsticks then grabs a pair for himself.

"Wow! This is a lot of food," I say looking at everything.

"I figured you be hungry and I didn't really know what you liked so I got a little of everything." He reaches for the Mongolian beef and puts a big helping on his plate then passes the carton to me.

I take it and put some on my plate along with some shrimp fried rice, a spring roll and a few crab puffs.

"Somebody's got an appetite," he says, eyeing my plate.

"You're one to talk. You put half the carton of Mongolian beef on your plate." I say with a laugh.

"I'm a growing boy. I need sustenance." He pats his belly playfully and I blush remembering how good the hard flesh of his stomach felt against my fingertips.

I wonder if what we did earlier is still on his mind. Neither of us has mentioned it although there is this underlying tension between us. A part of me wants to talk about what happened. About why he rejected me then left so abruptly but I'm not really sure I want to know the answer so I leave it alone.

"So, why are we staying the night here?" I ask before shoving a good helping of chow mien in my mouth.

"We figured it would be good for you to get away from Bradford for the night."

"We?" I ask.

"Me, Devya and Harlyn. We thought it best that you not go back to Bradford tonight."

"And why is that?" I ask, sitting my chopsticks down and training my gaze on him.

"Bexley is still pretty heated and she can be a hothead."

"I'm aware," I say, rolling my eyes. Since I'm gonna be here all night, did you at least bring my cell phone?" I ask, folding my arms across my chest. I've been at this cabin for hours with no communication with the outside world. This is the longest I've gone without a cell phone.

He stops eating and quirks and eyebrow at me.

I roll my eyes. "Since I have no cell phone I guess that means we get to talk. Spend some time getting to know each other." I say with a sarcastic smile.

He frowns and goes back to eating.

I take a few more bites of food then push my plate away.

"So," I begin. "Your grandfather left you this place. Were you two close?"

"Ummhmm," is all he says.

"When did he die?"

Zade's hand stills midair, a noodle dangles from his chopsticks. His jaw tightens as he looks over at me. Cleary talking about his grandfather is a sore subject for him.

I'm not a complete ass. The last thing I want to do is bring up sad memories. I wouldn't want anyone doing that to me. "I'm sorry. You don't have to talk about it if it's too hard. I know what it's like losing someone you love." My chest tightens as images of my mom surface. I swallow the pain before it crawls up my throat and releases itself like a tortured cat.

Zade lays his chopsticks on his plate. "He died last August," he says, his voice quiet.

"I'm sorry for your loss." My voice is just as quiet and my eyes are sad as I look at him. I lost someone very important to me and so did he. Maybe that's why I feel so connected to him.

"At least he left me all this and then some," he says, with a bitter chuckle.

"What do you mean?" I ask.

"The Amherst fortune, my grandfather left it all to me. He didn't leave my Dad shit and the old man is bitter as fuck about it."

There's an angry edge to him as he stares off to the side. I want to reach out and smooth away the tension straining his jawline.

"So you and your Dad don't get along?"

"Nah, not since my grandfather died. My Dad wants control of the family fortune and he has it for now. But, when I turn twenty-five it all comes to me. I'll be running everything."

"Maybe you two can work together. Share in the responsibilities," I suggest.

He looks at me, his eyes deadpan. "You don't know my father. He's not a sharer. And besides, he thinks I'm a big fuckup anyway. He's sure I'll lose the family fortune within a year of inheriting it."

"Why would he think that?"

"Cuz' he's a dick." he replies sharply.

I can see the tension gathering around his eyes. Clearly his father is a touchy subject. The last thing I want to do is make him upset so I steer the conversation in another direction.

"So, what's up with you and Indigo James?" I ask.

I can tell this question surprises him by the sidelong glance he gives me. "What do you mean?" He asks.

"I don't know. You two seem close. She's always hanging all over you. I was just wondering if you guys were a thing."

The corners of his mouth tilt up in amusement. "Nope," he says shaking his head.

"So, you guys never hooked up?"

"I didn't say that," he says, staring me in the eyes. He's being deliberately elusive, almost as if he's baiting me.

"Well what about the girl from the party?" I'm becoming more annoyed by the minute.

"What girl?" He questions with a frown.

"The girl you were screwing against the dresser," I say. I'm sure he can hear the disdain in my voice.

He drops his head and chuckles. "What about her?"

He's laughing at me and I don't like it. "Are you dating her?" There's definitely a clear bite of annoyance in my tone.

"I'm not dating anyone, Fallon" he says and stands up. He starts gathering up the food and takes it to the kitchen.

Normally I would help but I'm annoyed as fuck with him and his aloofness right now.

He comes back into the living room and sits down in the same armchair he occupied when we first arrived. "I see you finished all my bourbon."

"You left me here for hours. I got bored."

"It's cool. I have like two more bottles in the kitchen," he says.

"You Bradford kids sure like to drink," I say rather snidely.

"You do realize you're a Bradford kid too, right?" He says, cocking a brow, that beautiful mouth of his tilting up into a sexy grin.

Butterflies immediately skitter around in my stomach and I have to look away before I do something stupid like beg him to be with me again. Instead I decide to bait him. "I guess so. I mean I've already committed murder," I say, my voice seething with loathing.

The sexy grin fades and he shifts uncomfortably in his chair. "You're not a murderer, Fallon."

"Then what am I, Zade? Cuz' it kind of feels like I am." I look at him waiting for him to tell me otherwise.

He leans forward in his seat. "You're just a girl who's doing what she has to do to survive. You're in a den of wolves, Fallon. Nobody will blame you for protecting yourself."

"Or you and Bexley," I throw out.

"What are you saying?" He asks, his eyebrows drawing together in confusion.

"Me not saying anything about what we did the other night not only protects me - it protects you and Bexley too."

"I guess it does but we're not going to say anything either so I guess we're all protecting each other," he says then sits back in his chair.

Neither of us say anything after that. We just sit quietly each lost in our own thoughts for a while.

"I think I'll shower and call it a night." I grab the duffle bag and head down the hall.

Zade follows behind me. "Take the master bedroom. That bed is much more comfortable than the ones in any of the other rooms."

"Thanks," I say and go into the master bedroom and close the door.

I shower for a long time, letting the hot water rain down on me in hopes that it washes away all the bad times I've had since coming to Bradford. It helps a little I guess because the only thoughts running through my mind of are Zade and the feel of his lips on mine and the touch of his hands on my body. I want to feel them again.

I turn off the shower and get out, wrapping one of the big fluffy towels around me then step into the bedroom. I'm startled to find Zade standing at the dresser. He looks at me and his eyes immediately blaze fire.

Little goosebumps prickle my still damp skin and the place between my thighs tingles as I stare back at him. I press my thighs together to try and stop what's happening down there.

"Sorry. I keep all my clothes in here. I needed to grab a t-shirt," Zade says holding up a white shirt.

"It's fine," I say, the words coming out thick and a little choked.

He stares at me, his gaze heating my body as it travels over my face, down my throat and across my bare shoulders. The towel is wrapped tight around my body and stops just about mid-thigh but as he continues his ocular journey down my body I feel naked.

I think about dropping the towel. I want to but I'm not quite that bold so instead I take a tentative step towards him. I can see the pulse in his neck jump. I can feel the heat from his body calling to me. The air around us is so thick I can barely make my way through it and just as I reach him, he tears his gaze away and slams the drawer shut.

"Good night, Fallon," he says and hurries out the room.

I'm left standing alone, achy and needy. I know this boy is attracted to me. I can see it in his eyes, feel it in the air around us. I know what he said earlier. He thinks I want to be with him solely to dull the pain and I'm sure it will help with that but that's not why I want to be with him. I've been attracted to Zade since first laying eyes on him and now being here alone with him, getting to know more about him, makes me want him that much more.

CHAPTER NINETEEN

Zade and I don't talk much the next morning. We get up early and head back to Bradford. He drops me off at Barringer Hall and speeds away without a word.

I'm startled but not shocked to find Devya waiting for me in my room.

"Hey," she says running up and giving me a hug as soon as I open the door.

"Hey," I say hugging her back. "What are you doing here?"

"Zade messaged me. He said ya'll were heading back. I wanted to be here when you got home."

"How'd you get in?" I ask sitting the duffle bag down and kicking off my shoes.

She grabs her purse off the table and pulls out her keys. She holds up a hot pink key. "I have a skeleton key."

"A what?" I say, looking at her totally baffled.

"A skeleton key," she repeats looking at me like I'm a complete idiot.

"Don't look at me like that. I have no idea what a skeleton key is," I say, my cheeks heating with embarrassment.

"You're such a Martian sometimes, Fallon," she says with an amused smile.

She hands the key to me. It's shaped much different than any key I've ever seen. The serrated edges that are normally on keys are gone.

"That key," she says pointing to the key in my hand. "Will get me into almost any locked door here at Bradford."

"What! Where did you get this?" I ask looking at her in wonder.

She snatches the key out of my hand. "Let's just say, I'm well connected." She winks and places the key back in her purse.

She grabs my hand and pulls me over to the sofa to sit down. Her face turning serious. "So, how are you?" She asks.

"I'm fine," I say even though that's a lie. I'm actually still feeling some type of way about the fire but I guess I always will. I'm also feeling some type of way about Zade Amherst, our make-out session, him seeing me in only a towel and him barely looking at me this morning.

"Good. I have to ask, are you still thinking about going to the police?"

"No," I say with a sigh.

"What changed your mind? Was it Zade?" She asks, searching my face.

"He may have shed some light on the situation."

"How so?"

"I don't know. I guess he made me realize that I don't want to go to jail for possibly the rest of my life. I feel shitty even thinking it but I'm seventeen. There is so much that I still want to do with my life and I can't do that behind bars." I stare down at my hands. Even though I've made up my mind, I feel like such a coward.

"You're making the right decision, Fallon," Devya says, placing her hand over mine reassuringly. "Now get dressed. We have twenty minutes before first period.

"Oh my gosh, I'm starving," Devya says as we make our way out of math class and head towards the dining hall.

This morning's classes seemed to fly by. Zade was M.I.A. from chemistry and the rest of the pure bloods were oddly quiet. Indigo, Tatum and Chloe barely registered me a glance in class. It was kind of nice being under the radar.

Lucca and Harlyn are already in the dining hall when me and Devya get there. Harlyn waves us over.

"What's up, chic? You good?" Harlyn says as I sit down.

"I'm cool," I say giving her a reassuring smile. I cut my eyes over at Lucca who's full on staring at me, his brown eyes penetrating and giving me that whimsical giddy feeling.

"Hey, Lucca," I say.

He just nods then picks up his menu and starts reading it.

"They have truffle mac-n-cheese today," Devya says with a moan.

"Settle down, tiger. We don't need you having an orgasm at the table," Harlyn says with a smirk.

"I bet this mac-n-cheese can give me a better orgasm then you could any day," Devya says, mischief dancing in her eyes.

Harlyn turns in her seat and opens her legs. She grabs Devya's chair pulling it between her thighs then tip-toes her fingertips up Devya's bare thigh. "You wanna bet," Harlyn says, her tone low and flirty.

Devya raises a brow in challenge.

"Damn, you bitches are hot!" Alisander says bounding over to the table. He bends down putting his face in between Harlyn and Devya's. "I don't know what ya'll got going on but mind if I join in."

"You're such a dick, Sander," Harlyn says pushing him upside the head.

"What? I just want to be a part of the female experience. Learn what it is you all like so I can elevate my sex game," he says, feigning innocence.

Devya throws her head back in laughter and moves her seat so she's facing the table again.

Alisander comes around the table and pulls out the chair next to me and sits down. "How's our little arson? Still planning on singing like a bird?'" He asks, his mouth quirked up at the corners, his eyes teasing.

"Knock it off, Alisander. It's too soon for jokes," Devya chastises.

Alisander puts his hands up in surrender. "Hey, I was just checking the temperature of things. Making sure I don't need to call up my family's fancy lawyer to help out. This one here seems a bit unpredictable."

I whip my head in his direction. "What does that mean?"

"It's really cute the way your nose scrunches up like that when you're annoyed," he says tweaking my nose and not bothering to address my question.

I swat his hand away and he laughs.

"Why are you always teasing me?" I ask him.

He leans in. "Maybe you're growing on me. And you are pretty hot so..."

Lucca, who's sitting one seat over from Alisander lets out a low growl. He's been so quiet this whole time I almost forgot he was there.

Alisander ignores him and leans in closer to me, his warm breath fanning my face. He smells good, like a tropical island - coconuts and exotic fruits. He's nothing like Zade who is dark and brooding with that overwhelmingly addictive black licorice and cola smell, no, Alisander's scent is light, fun and dizzying. It matches his character perfectly - playfully zipping through life like it's one big party. He just makes you want to have a good time. I have to admit, it's infectious.

"Seriously! Why is it that every time I turn around this bitch is all up in your face?"

My hackles go up as I turn to see Bexley standing behind us, hand on her hip, full, painted lips twisted into the ugliest scowl.

The mood at the table immediately shifts as tension fills the space.

"Chill out, Bex. We're just having a little fun. You should join us," Alisander says motioning for her to sit down.

"As if I'd share a table with her low rent ass. She doesn't belong here. I don't know why you guys don't see that," she spits, her ice blue eyes frosting over. She moves in closer and before I know it she's grabbed a junk of my hair and yanks my head back. "You may have them all fooled but not me. Just know, I'll end you before I let you fuck up what I have here."

She did it so fast no one had any time to react. My scalps on fire from the death grip she has on my hair. I yelp and reach up, clawing at her hand.

"Alisander!" Devya yells. "Stop her."

Alisander jumps up and wraps his arm around Bexley's waist. "C'mon, babe, enough. I think she gets the picture," he coaxes but Bexley's not listening to him. Her focus is on me.

She tightens her grip on my hair and raises her other hand. I just know she's going to slap or punch me.

"Bexley, enough!" Harlyn yells as she jumps up. She races around the table and grabs Bexley's arm stopping her from hitting me. With her other hand she pries my hair free and I jump up from the table.

My heart is pounding and my adrenaline is on ten. My body is shaking with rage as I stare at Bexley. I lunge at her but Lucca's there in a heartbeat standing between us. I slam into his hard body and he wraps his arms around my waist hugging me to him.

"Let me go," I seethe. If I have to tussle with this bitch every time we're in the same room so be it. I'm more than tired of her shit.

"Unh-uh, let's go," he says ushering me towards the exit.

I squirm trying to get out of his grasp but he just tightens his grip and lifts me off my feet and carries me out of the dining hall.

"Lucca, put me down. I can walk by myself," I yell shoving against his chest.

The few kids in the hallway stop and stare at us but Lucca doesn't put me down until we're outside in the courtyard. And he doesn't just put me down. He sits down in one of the dining chairs and pulls me down in his lap so I'm straddling him.

I'm angry but the feel of his firm thighs against the soft flesh of my bottom is distracting. Not to mention the fact that I'm straddling him. It's a good thing the courtyard is empty.

"Fallon," he says, grabbing me by the chin and forcing me to look at him. "Calm down. You have to stop letting Bexley get you all worked up."

"What are you talking about? You're just as crazy as the rest of them when it comes to Bexley. She comes after me every chance she gets and you want me to calm down." I'm completely exasperated. These kids are nuts. One behaves badly and they all just accept it. I don't understand it all.

"That's Bexley. She's always been like that. There's no point in trying to change her. But you..." he pauses, grabbing a strand of my hair and rubbing it between his fingers. "You're not like her. You're a better person than her."

My heart skips as I look at him. His brown eyes glitter with kindness edged in need. His body tightens beneath me as he stares up at me and I can't help but run my hands up his corded arms, liking the feel of how his muscles ripple underneath my fingers.

"I probably shouldn't be sitting on you like this. Someone could see us out here," I breathe out.

"I don't care," he says gripping my hips and pulling me further up his lap.

I gasp feeling the bulge in his pants settle into the crevice of my ass and I forget all about Bexley and being angry. I stare down into his beautiful face - and it is beautiful. In fact, it's as close to perfection as any boy's face can get. I spend a moment admiring it. The light brown eyes, the perfectly natural shaped and glossy eyebrows, the angular jaw, the full lips. I lower my head until my lips hover half an inch above his. His lips part slightly and our breaths mingle. I want to kiss him but I hesitate remembering we're out in public.

Lucca lifts his chin to connect our mouths but I place my fingers against his lips stopping him.

"We're in public," I remind him again.

"So," he says, his lips soft against my fingers.

"I thought you didn't want anyone to see us together."

"Yeah, well, I guess I don't care anymore." He grabs my wrist and gently removes my finger from his mouth.

We stare at each other for a few seconds before closing the distance and allowing our lips to touch. The kiss is soft, sweet at first as he nibbles on my bottom lip then top lip before slipping his tongue inside my mouth. Our tongues dance around each other and I wrap my hands around his neck and interlace my fingers. His grip tightens on my hips and he starts to gently rock me back and forth across his erection. The feeling is mind-blowing causing tiny little explosions to go off in my body. I can feel the spot between my thighs moisten. As things heat up the kiss between us becomes more urgent. I rub and massage his shoulders and find myself rocking harder against him as I let out little moans of pleasure.

"Stop...stop," Lucca says against my mouth. He tightens his grip on my hips holding them in place, stilling my movements.

I look down at him through lust-hazed eyes, my breaths coming out short and heavy. "What? Why?" I pant.

"Because like you said, we're in public and you're about to make me cum," he whispers against my lips.

I inhale sharply at his words and my eyes grow big in surprise.

He chuckles. "What did you think would happen? You're straddling me and grinding against me."

"I'm sorry," I say, my cheeks flushing pink. I look nervously around the courtyard. What is it about these Bradford boys? They got me acting completely out of character. I've already gone way further with Lucca and Zade then I've gone with any boy my entire seventeen years.

"Don't worry, no one's out here but you and me." He runs his finger along my cheek sending a new series of tingles throughout my body.

I can't continue to sit on him like this. All it's doing is keeping me worked up. "I should get up."

He stares at me for a few moments then releases my hips. I stand on wobbly legs and step back a few feet. Lucca stands up as well and the bulge in his pants is clearly evident. I can't lie it's exciting to know that I'm the cause of it.

He takes a few steps towards me closing the distance I put between us. He reaches out, fingering a few strands of my hair. He really likes doing that.

"I really do like you, Fallon," he says.

"I like you too, Lucca."

"Do you?" He asks which I find odd.

"I mean, I *was* just straddling you in the middle of the court-yard." I say with a wry smile.

"True," he says nodding his head. "But, you went off with Zade yesterday."

Well that caught me off guard. I did not expect him to say that. "Well, yeah, but you heard what happened, right?"

"Yeah, I heard a little bit. You had a run-in with Bexley and Zade got you out of there before you two killed each other."

"Basically. It seems like someone is always pulling me away from that girl," I say, shaking my head.

"And where did he take you?" He asks his face serious, intense.

Suddenly my throat is dry and it's hard to swallow. I know where this line of questioning is going and I'm nervous. "We went somewhere private, away from everyone. He thought I needed a break from Bradford."

"Did you spend the night with him?" Lucca asks, the muscles in his jaw tightening.

"Yeah, but not like you think." My nerves skitter through my body and my belly hollows out as I stare at him.

"What do I think, Fallon? Tell me." He says shoving his hands in his pockets.

"I think you think that we slept together but we didn't." I say.

"So, what did you do?"

"We talked, ate, and drank a little bit..."

"Did you fool around?" He asks looking me square in the eyes.

A twinge of guilt hits me as I look at him. I could lie and tell him that nothing happened but the way he's looking at me I know he won't believe me. The crazy thing is that I really don't want to lie to him. I really do like him but I also like Zade and hell there's even some sort of attraction brewing with Alisander. These three boys have got me all off kilter right now. I have no idea what I'm doing. I just know that I like how they make me feel.

"We messed around a little but we didn't have sex," I admit.

"Do you like him?"

I can't lie to him. "Yes, but I like you too."

Lucca drops his head and runs his hand across the top of his head and down the back of his neck. "Damn, Fallon, I should probably walk away now but there's just something about you."

He grabs the waistband of my skirt and pulls me to him. He stares down at me and the intensity of his gaze is startling. There in the depths of his eyes is passion, longing, protection. No guy has ever looked at me like that. It's overwhelming but I like it.

The connection I have with Lucca is completely different than the connection I have with Zade. Each guy stirs something different in me. What I feel with Lucca is a slow simmer. A steady build-up that I know will end in the most beautifully explosive way. With Zade there's a dark, intensity. It's lust and fireworks. It's desperation and hunger when we're together. An intoxicating push, pull that gets my blood pumping and sets my soul on fire. Zade is all consuming and there's no balance. It's either all flames or total burnout. I'm caught between a soft ember and a blazing inferno and I want them both equally.

CHAPTER TWENTY

Weeks have gone by and summer has more than officially made way to fall. We're in Texas so that's not saying all that much. It's still hot as hell outside but football season is in full swing and Bradford has its first home game this weekend.

Things have calmed down a bit with Bexley. She still gives me dirty looks and never misses an opportunity to put me down but at least she's laid off the physical attacks. Her minions, Indigo, Tatum and Chloe basically follow her lead so I haven't had any issue with them either. I just do my best to steer clear of those hens.

I'm still tutoring Lucca, or at least trying to. We spend most of the hour making out and talking instead of studying. We talk about football quite a bit as well. Bradford's first four games were away games so he's really excited for the first home game. He's stopped taking the steroids and hasn't missed a beat. He's still fast, strong and showing out on the field.

While Lucca and I are getting closer, I haven't seen much of Zade. It's like he's deliberately avoiding me since we got back from his cabin. He shows up to chemistry class just as the bell rings and makes sure to sit as far away from me as possible. In art class, he wears air pods the entire time and doesn't look my way once. It's so frustrating because even though he's ignoring me his scent plays at my nostrils whenever he's near and I'm reminded of being kissed by his expert lips and touched and caressed by those experienced hands of his. I want to confront him and ask him why he's avoiding me but if I'm honest I'm afraid of the answer, so I don't.

I've just finished getting dressed when there's a knock at my door.

"Open up, Trick!" Harlyn's yells playfully through the door.

We're meeting Devya at the dining hall for dinner then heading over to the football game.

"Don't you look like a little hottie," Harlyn says sweeping past me as I open the door.

"Thanks," I say looking down at my outfit. I'm wearing a pair of designer distressed jeans and a cropped hoodie. I straightened my hair and put it up in a high ponytail, leaving out a few tendrils to frame my face. My makeup is minimal, just some mascara, eyeliner and some gloss for my lips.

Harlyn on the other hand looks amazing. I swear she looks like she stepped right out of some alternative magazine where the models wear all black clothing and dark makeup. She's wearing a cropped AC/DC t-shirt, distressed black skinny jeans and combat boots. Her makeup is sick with the dark sultry eyes, long, thick faux lashes, and black lipstick. She's a total rock star and I love it.

"I look like a plain Jane compared to you, Harlyn," I pout.

"Not even. We just have different aesthetics. That's all. Now let's go. I'm starving." She throws her arm around my shoulder and we head out.

Devya's already in the dining hall when we arrive. In fact, the dining hall is way more packed than it usually is for dinner. Kids normally order in or go out to eat for dinner.

"Why is it so packed in here tonight?" I ask as we sit down.

"Game night. Almost everybody eats in the dining hall when we have home games. It's just easier. You eat and walk over to the football field right after," Devya says.

"Let's see what's on the menu tonight," Harlyn says sitting down. A big shit-eating grin gracing her lips. "I love it when we have home games. Look at this menu," she says leaning over and showing me the menu.

I look at the menu. It's all junk food - pizza, burgers, fries, and milkshakes. Every item has the word gourmet in front of it but it's junk food nonetheless. Harlyn and I order the gourmet cheeseburger and fries and Devya gets a pizza.

"We're riding to the party together after the game, right?" Devya asks her eyes glued to her cell phone.

"Duh," Harlyn replies.

"What party?" I ask clearly out of the loop.

Devya looks up from her cell phone frowning. "How can you still be so out of the loop, Fallon? There's a party tonight at Alisander's after the game."

"I don't know. I guess I'm not a part of the group chat where these party announcements happen." I shrug.

"Aren't you on social media?" She asks.

"Yeah, but I don't use it much."

"Well there's your problem. Alisander announces all of his parties on Insta. Give me your phone," she demands holding out her hand.

I unlock my phone and hand it to her.

She spends a few minutes swiping and tapping before handing it back to me, a satisfied smile on her face. "There! You now follow the who's who of Bradford and a couple of kids over at Elmsley. Now you'll be clued in on what's going on. And don't worry, they'll follow you back soon. In fact, you'll probably be getting a bunch of new follows soon."

"Why do you say that?" I see no reason why anybody would want to follow me on social media. I rarely post anything.

She gives me an annoyed look. "Because you're Fallon Fucking Gamble and you're one of *us* - a Pure Blood. Besides, I'm going to start tagging you in my posts which will up your social media stock dramatically." She shoves her phone in my face. "I've got over forty thousand followers."

"Wow! That's a lot." I cringe thinking about how my low follower count. I think I may have nine hundred followers the last time I checked.

"I know right. You'll probably surpass me soon. Your stock is on the rise, girl," she says with a wink.

Our food arrives and we eat pretty quickly then head over to the stadium. My cell phone buzzes just as we're heading inside. It's a text from Lucca asking me to meet him by the locker room door that's off the back parking lot. I'm not sure what he wants but I agree.

"You guys go ahead. I have to run to the bathroom," I say.

"Are you sure you want to go alone?" Harlyn asks, her brow cocked.

"I should be fine. Bexley and the rest of the hens have been leaving me alone lately.

Harlyn and Devya exchange looks as if they're not sure.

"I'll be fine. If I see Bexley I'll run the other way," I joke.

"Fine. But if you're not out back in ten minutes, were coming to look for you," Devya says.

"Fine, mom," I say, pretending to be annoyed.

They laugh and make their way into the stadium. I head towards the back parking lot.

Lucca's waiting for me outside the locker room door. He's leaning against the wall, one leg bent and resting against the building, helmet hanging from his hand at his side. He looks good as shit in his uniform. The way the uniform pants hug his thighs revealing just how sturdy and muscular they are, has my mouth watering.

"Hey," I say as I reach him.

His eyes light up at seeing me. He doesn't say anything, he just sits his helmet on the ground, pulls me into his arms and buries his face in my neck. I wrap my arms around him, hugging him back. He smells like soap and fresh sweat. It's actually a heady combination.

"Is everything okay?" I ask, concern creeping in. I hope he's not going to tell me that he slipped up and started using steroids again.

"I'm fine," he says pulling back and looking me in the eyes.

"I just wanted to see you before the game. It's the first home game. My nerves are little all over the place."

I run my fingers along the soft hairs at the back of his neck and smile. "You're going to be great. You're Lucca Caldwell, one of the top high school running backs in the country."

"Yeah, that's what has me all nerved up. Expectations to win this first home game are high as hell. Coach has been riding me and let's not even talk about my Dad. I can't make one mistake tonight," he says shaking his head.

I brace my hands on either side of his face. "Listen to me. You're gonna be amazing and me and Harlyn and Devya will be in the stands cheering you on."

"Thank you. It's funny. I've only known you a few months and you've given me more support than the people I've known my whole life. I know moving to Texas and coming to Bradford has been hard for you but I'm glad you're here, Fallon." He looks down at me, sheer wonder in his eyes, before dipping his head and pressing his lips to mine. I open up for him right away sliding my tongue against his. His hands roam my body moving from my back to my waist and down to my butt. The kiss is getting pretty heated. I find myself pressing into him as I let out little moans of pleasure. Our breathing is ragged and heavy when we finally break apart.

"I gotta go," he says, resting his forehead against mine.

"Okay," I nod. "Have a good game."

He steps back and picks up his helmet. "I'll see you at the party later," he says before disappearing into the building.

My skin is all warm and tingly as I walk back to the front entrance of the stadium. I don't fully know what's going on with me and Lucca Caldwell but I like it.

I see Devya and Harlyn as soon as I enter the stadium. They're sitting midway up the bleachers at the fifty yard line. Alisander, Bexley, Indigo, Tatum and Chloe are sitting in the same row as them. Devya waves me over. I brace myself for a verbal onslaught from Bexley about how I don't belong with them but surprisingly she just ignores me.

The atmosphere in the stadium is crazy. The place is packed with students, faculty and parents. It's so loud that you can barely hear when the commentator announces the start of the game.

Bradford gets the ball first and takes full advantage of it. Lucca runs for twenty yards on Bradford's first possession and scores a touch-down on the very next possession. The crowd goes wild. I'm so proud of him, I'm beaming.

"You a huge football fan?" Harlyn asks.

"Eh. Why do you ask?" I say my eyes glued to the game - glued to Lucca.

"The way you're smiling and cheering a person would think you love the game or you're dating someone on the team," she says eyeing me.

I whip my head around and look at her. "What? Why would you say that?" My voice sounds pitchy as hell. *Shit! I know I sound guilty.*

Harlyn's mouth splits into a sly smile and she narrows her eyes at me. "I'm on to you, Nebraska."

"What are you talking about? There's nothing to be on to," I say waving her off.

"Yeah, whatever. Lucca stares at you all day, you disappear right before the game and you out here cheering for him like you're his own personal one woman cheerleading squad. C'mon," she says giving me a side eye.

"Fine," I say leaning over to whisper in her ear. "We've been hanging out."

"You and Lucca Caldwell. I can see that," she says nodding.

"So what else have ya'll been up to besides hanging out." She throws up air quotes when she says hanging out.

"Nothing really. It's not even serious. We've made out a few times that's all. You know kissing and a little grinding here and there but that's it."

The look Harlyn's giving me tells me that she doesn't believe me at all.

"Seriously. That's all we've done." I say.

"Because it's you I'll believe what you're saying but I've known Lucca for a long time and he doesn't just make out with chics. The boy is a lady killer. I've heard some good things about his... assets. If you ever do anything other than kiss and grind, rumor has it that you'll be very satisfied."

"Harlyn!" I say bumping her with my arm.

"Hey, don't shoot the messenger," she laughs.

Just as we focus back on the game, Lucca makes another touchdown. The guys on fire. I'm sure his father will be very proud of the way his son played tonight.

The after party at Alisander's lake house is off the chain. The place is packed wall to wall with Bradford kids and there's quite a few kids from the school we beat in tonight's game.

"This party is lit! Let's dance," Harlyn says as soon as we enter the house. She grabs me and Devya's hand and pulls us into the crowd of gyrating bodies.

The dance floor is hot, sweaty and sticky as hell. The DJ is spinning nothing but hits and we're all going crazy on the dance floor. I'm having so much fun. Boys, Bexley and the fire are far from my mind and I like it.

"Oh my gawd! I'm dying. It's so hot. Come outside with me for a second," Devya yells over the music.

"You guys go. I'm about to roll up on Lacy Fitzpatrick and see what she's talking about," Harlyn says that playboy grin splitting her mouth in half.

Devya and I just look at each other, shake our heads then head for the front entrance.

The air outside is cooler than the inferno we just left on the dance floor but it's still rather warm out.

"Man that DJ is really showing out tonight. I love it." Devya says, fanning herself.

"He really is. And I'm actually having a lot of fun tonight," I confess.

"Really, Fallon? That's awesome. I told you we're not that bad."

I level my stare at her. "Oh, ya'll are terrible. It's just that ya'll haven't done anything shitty tonight," I laugh.

"Shut up!" Devya says hitting me playfully on the arm.

"Real talk, tonight is the first time I'm not spending the whole night wondering when Bexley's gonna come for me. It's nice to not have to watch my back all the time, you know."

Devya nods. "I bet. I just hope things remain cool."

"Me too."

"Devya, what's up? I been looking for you." We turn to see Cord Michelson coming out the front door.

"Oh, hey, Cord," Devya says her shoulders immediately tensing up.

"Hey, yourself. Where have you been? I feel like you've been dodging me," he says looking seriously hurt.

"It's not like that. I've just been really busy," Devya says looking everywhere but at Cord.

I feel like a six toe standing here while they have this very personal and very awkward conversation. I decide to back away and give them some space. I'm not ready to go back inside so I head towards the driveway. No one is out here so I figure I'm good.

I walk a few yards. Strategically placed yard lights help to partially light up the driveway but for the most part it's dark which is why I'm startled when I walk up on Zade leaning casually against his motorcycle smoking a blunt.

"Oh my gosh! You scared me. I didn't you see over here." I say, pressing my palm to my thundering heart.

He just looks at me, those blue-violet eyes piercing as he takes a long pull on his blunt, holds the smoke in for several long moments then slowly releases it from him mouth. *Jeezus! The boy even makes smoking look sexy.*

"What are you doing out here in the dark by yourself?" He asks.

"Devya and I came outside to get some fresh air."

"Looks to me like you're by yourself." He takes another pull on his blunt. My eyes watch his mouth. I can't help it.

He lifts his foot and smashes the blunt against his shoe, snuffing out the fire then tucks the blunt behind his ear.

"Devya's on the porch talking to Cord. He feels like she's been ignoring him. The conversation was getting uncomfortable so I figured I'd give them some space."

"And you thought you'd walk out here alone, in the dark instead of going inside," he says, narrowing his gaze at me.

"I guess when you put it like that, it wasn't my best idea. But do you care? You haven't talked to me since we left your cabin," I accuse.

I notice a slight twitch in his jaw but it's gone just as quickly as it happened. "We never really talked before the cabin so I don't see what the problem is."

There's a slight tightening of my heart at that comment. He really just doesn't care and that sucks because I'm really starting to have feelings for him. His nonchalance is really annoying. "Of course, you don't see a problem, Zade. Apparently, girls are like toys to you. You play with them for a little bit then toss them aside."

"You don't know what you're talking about," he says, his voice low, even.

"I know we had a connection at your cabin. I know that you felt something when we kissed, and yet, for some reason you're back to acting like I don't exist." I'm raising my voice and I don't even realize it.

"Go back inside, Fallon," Zade says, his eyes just as serious as his voice.

There's something about the way that he's looking at me that tells me I should listen. I should turn around and go inside but my legs won't move. "Make me," I say taunting him.

His eyes narrow to slits and that beautiful mouth flattens to an angry line before he grabs me and crushes my mouth with his. My arms wrap around his neck immediately and I mold my body to his. The kiss is hard and hungry. A clashing of tongues and teeth as we flick and twirl our tongues around each other.

His black licorice and cola scent engulfs me causing my brain to cloud and my heart to flutter. I press my body closer to his - as close as humanly possible and I get swept up in everything Zade Amherst.

Zade pulls back from the kiss abruptly, leaving me surprised and wanting. My breathing is shallow and my heart is beating so fast you'd think I just ran a 5k race.

"Go inside, Fallon," Zade says, the words coming out thick and short between heavy breaths. He doesn't wait for me to respond or move. He hops on his bike, starts it up and speeds off, leaving me standing there, staring desperately after him.

CHAPTER
TWENTY ONE

I make my way back to the house on shaky legs, my body and mind still reeling from the kiss with Zade. Devya and Cord are no longer on the porch. Hopefully, they're off somewhere working out their issues.

Me, I need to get myself together before I go back to the party so I head down a hallway in the opposite direction of the party in search of a bathroom so I can collect myself.

The hallway is endless and is lined with several doors. As I make my way down the hall I open the doors and peek inside looking to see if any of them are bathrooms. I'm halfway down the hall and haven't run into a bathroom yet. As I get further down the hall I hear a male voice and whoever it is, is not happy. There's a violent sting in his tone as he speaks.

The voice is coming from one of the rooms at near the end of the hall and as I make my way further down the hallway the voice gets louder, clearer. The door to one of the rooms is slightly ajar and I peek inside to see Alisander pacing and speaking angrily into his cell phone.

"I know, Father. I get it. You're right! All I do is party and I don't take anything seriously. Maybe you should marry another twenty-two year old and have another kid so you can leave your precious fortune to him," he yells then chucks the phone across the room.

This is a side of Alisander I've never seen. He's always very cool and jokey. He can be a bit of an ass at times but overall, he's a fun-loving guy who likes to have a good time.

"You okay?" I ask stepping into the room.

He whips around a look of surprise framing his gorgeous face. "What are you doing down here?" He asks frowning.

"I was looking for a bathroom," I say nervously. I clearly walked in on a private moment.

"There's one over there," he says pointing to a door across the room.

"Thanks," I say and make my way over there. I can feel Alisander's eyes on me and I quicken my pace, hurrying to the bathroom and closing the door.

The nerves rattling my body from my encounter with Zade have faded and shifted into concern for Alisander. He sounded really angry on the phone with his father. I take a minute to check over my appearance in the mirror. The lip-gloss I was wearing is completely gone which I'm sure is thanks to Zade Amherst. I pull the tube of gloss out of my pocket and reapply it to my lips, take a deep breath then leave the bathroom.

Alisander is standing next to the large window at the far end of the room. His back is to me and I can tell from the soft set of his shoulders and the way his head is hanging that he's not doing well.

I walk over to him, my footsteps silent against the plush carpet. "Hey," I say coming up behind him.

He doesn't say anything and he doesn't turn around.

I move to the side so I'm facing him. He's still looking out the window but he can see me out of his peripheral.

"Do you want to talk about it?" I ask. Even in a down mood, I can't help but notice how gorgeous he is with his thick mop of flaxen colored hair, flawless skin and kissable lips. His clothes are expensive and definitely designer but he's still rocking that effortlessly disheveled look.

"Not really. It's just the same old typical family bullshit, you know," his voice is heavy and his eyes stay trained out the window.

"Actually, I don't know. I had a pretty good relationship with my mom. She was amazing really." I say, my voice catching a little as I think of her.

Alisander turns to face me, those grey eyes of his softening a bit. "I almost forgot you didn't grow up like I did. I bet your mom was supportive and didn't burden you with family money and legacy bullshit."

"She always stressed the importance of family but never as if it was a burden."

"Figures. I bet being poor is so much easier than having more money than you know what to do with," he scowls.

"Being poor has its own set of burdens, Alisander."

"Maybe," he says, sliding his hands in his pockets and eyeing me. "You know there are like three bathrooms near the front of the house where the party is, right?"

"Are there?" I ask, knowing good and well that there are.

"Yes, yet you came all the way back here looking for a bathroom?" His eyebrows lift in question.

I bite my lip and shift my gaze away from him.

"Oh, no you don't. What's the deal? Who are you running from? Bexley?"

"No, she's actually been leaving me alone lately, thank God." I say.

"Then who? Lucca?" he asks, the corners of his mouth lifting in a knowing smirk.

"What? No! Why would you say that?" I sound totally defensive and the bright coloring of me cheeks are sure to give me away.

"I know he likes you. He stares at you all the time and I saw ya'll in the courtyard that day Bexley came for you."

As if I wasn't already embarrassed enough, my cheeks flame a brighter red and my entire body heats up. "You saw us?"

"Yep, and ya'll put on a pretty good show too. I was a little turned on," he jokes.

I punch him playfully on the arm. "You're such a jerk."

"I know. I can't help myself. But, seriously, you're hot as shit, Fallon. And you're sweet too. You can really make a guy fall for you, you know that?"

His expression turns serious as he looks at me and the air around us electrifies. Alisander has flirted with me and teased me plenty of times but there's something about the way he's looking at me now that's more than just a flirtation.

"I can't lie. Seeing you two together made me a little jealous," he admits and I'm completely shocked.

"Why would you be jealous? You don't even like me," I say putting my hands on my hips. "And, aren't you and Bexley a thing?" I add.

He frowns. "First of all, who says I don't like you?"

"Your actions and the way you make fun of me says you don't like me."

"To be fair, none of us liked you when you first came here. You're a bastard, an outsider. You showing up really fucked up the hierarchy around here," he says as if that makes it okay.

"See, that's why I say you don't like me. You just referred to me as a bastard, Alisander."

"But that's what you are. You were born out of wedlock thus you're a bastard," he reasons.

Okay, he's not wrong but man that term really stings. "I get it but people just don't go around calling people bastards all willy-nilly. It's rude."

"I guess but it doesn't matter anymore anyway. You're one of us now." He reaches out and brushes a tendril of hair out of my face. His knuckles brush my cheek leaving a sweet, tingly sensation in their wake.

I'll be damned if those stupid butterflies don't start dancing in my belly again. What is wrong with me? How can I be this attracted to three different guys?

"I want to kiss you," Alisander says moving in close, his coconut scent tickling my nose. "Can I kiss you, Fallon?"

I can't even find my voice to respond. All I know is that I'm hot all over and my stomach feels like it's about to fall out of my butt. When he puts his finger under my chin and lifts my head up, I don't stop him. In fact, I'm squealing with anticipation on the inside as I watch his head descend towards mine. He's going to kiss me and I want him to so bad but he doesn't right away. His eyes fall to my lips and linger for a moment before gently pressing against mine. His kiss is soft, searching as he runs his mouth along the seam of my lips before parting them and with the slowest movement, sliding his tongue inside. Alisander's kiss is what romance novels are made of. It starts out tender and builds to an urgent tempo where tongues duel, hands are everywhere and all rational thought goes out the window.

It's early Monday morning and I'm on my way to see Professor Blackmore. It's not even 7am and it's already scorching hot out. I'm still waiting for real fall weather to show up. If I was in Nebraska it would be about twenty degrees with a hundred percent chance of snow in the afternoon.

"Good Morning, Fallon," Professor Blackmore says as I walk into his office.

"Morning," I say sounding much chipper than I ever have since I started seeing him.

He raises an eyebrow. "You're in a good mood this morning. Did something happen?"

"I think it's just that I'm finally settling in here. Things were pretty rocky when I first got here." I say.

"And things are going well now?" He asks, his pen poised over his notebook.

"Let's just say they're going much better than they were. The kids here are starting to accept me." And it's true. I had such a terrible start here at Bradford but after the Dare Party things started looking up. Well, they did after I decided not to go the police about the fire that killed Dieter Calais. I'm sure it'll come back to haunt me one day but for now I've found a way to bury it. And because of that there have been no new physical attacks by Bexley or the other girls, no one's called me Stray for a while and I've been making out with the three hottest guys at Bradford. I'd say things are looking up.

Professor Blackmore jots something down in his notebook. "I'm happy for you, Fallon. You've been through a lot so it's nice that you're starting to feel comfortable here at Bradford.

After finishing my session with Professor Blackmore, I meet up with Devya and Harlyn and we walk to first period together.

"Man, that party was crazy," Harlyn says. She's walking backwards and I'm seriously nervous that she's going to run into something or someone.

"Would you turn around and walk normally like the rest of us please," I say, frowning at her.

She rolls her eyes and keeps walking backwards. "I want to see your faces while I talk to you."

"You're nuts," I laugh.

"Guess who I hooked up with at the party?" Harlyn asks, looking from me to Devya.

"I don't know," I say.

"Devya!" Harlyn shouts. "Get your nose out of that damn phone. I'm trying to brag here."

"Everything's not always about you, Harlyn!" Devya shouts her brows furrowing in anger.

Both Harlyn and I stare at Devya in shock.

"Hey, are you okay," I ask, placing my hand on her shoulder.

She throws her head to the sky and lets out a tortured sigh. "Cord just message me. The news just broke the story about his father. He's devastated. He needs to talk to someone and he says I'm the only one he trusts." She fixes her tortured gaze on me and Harlyn. "You guys. I'm the one who did this. He can't trust me."

"He doesn't know that you were the one who leaked that story, D. And trust me none of us will ever tell him so he'll never know."

"But I know. He's a good guy, Harlyn. He doesn't deserve to be lied to," Devya says.

"Cord is a good dude," Harlyn agrees. "If it's too much for you, end things. Then you won't have to be around him and you won't feel guilty."

"I really like him. I don't want to end things," she says dropping her head in sorrow.

I feel so bad for Devya. If it wasn't for that damn Dare Party she wouldn't be going through this. I wish I had words of encouragement for her but who am I to give her advice? I have my own secrets.

"Let's just go to class," Devya says and starts walking.

Harlyn and I exchange a concerned look before falling in step with her. We walk Devya to her first period class then I head to chemistry and Harlyn heads to math class.

I take my usual seat at the front of the room and scroll through my Instagram while I wait for the bell to ring. I'm shocked when I go to my page and see that I have two thousand new followers. I guess Devya was right.

Tatum and Chloe walk in and head straight to the back. Indigo and Zade aren't with them which is odd. I get a nasty knot in the pit of my stomach. Are they off somewhere together hooking up - having sex? I nearly throw up at the thought. Thank goodness a few minutes later Indigo comes storming into the classroom looking pissed off. I deliberately look down to avoid any possible eye contact with her. A few minutes later Zade strolls in but instead of heading to the back of the room and sitting with Indigo, he takes a seat in the front on the far side of the room. I'm not sure what's going on with Zade and Indigo but I can't say I'm not pleased that he's not sitting with her today.

Devya's waiting for me after chemistry so we can walk to French class together. She doesn't talk much as we walk to class which is completely out of character for her but I know she's going through some things so I just walk quietly next to her hoping that my presence provides her some comfort.

"Yo!" Alisander calls to us as we're about to enter the classroom.

My face instantly flushes as I remember the amazing kiss we shared at the party.

"What's up, Sander?" Devya says, looking annoyed.

"You guys didn't hear?" He asks, looking alarmed.

"Hear what?" I ask.

He focuses his gaze on me. There's a certain level of angst in his stare and I immediately panic.

"Hear what, Alisander?" I ask again.

"There's a detective on campus. She's investigating the death of Dieter Calais.

My blood goes cold and there's a sudden heaviness in my chest. The entire world around me goes fuzzy and I think I stop breathing.

"Fallon, are you okay?" Devya says bracing her hands on my shoulder.

I know she's talking but I can't comprehend the words.

"She looks like she's in shock. Let's take her to the courtyard and get her some air," Alisander says.

They usher me down the hall. I know I'm moving but everything seems so surreal right now. The only thing I can seem to focus on is the fact that there's a detective investigating the death of Dieter Calais and she's on campus.

When we get to the courtyard they sit me down in a chair. Devya's using her bag to fan me and Alisander is kneeling in front of me.

"Fallon, you good?" Alisander asks.

I just stare at him, in shock, terrified and unable to speak.

He places a hand on my knee. "I need you to talk to me. Now's not the time to check out, baby girl."

"There ya'll are," Lucca says bursting through the doors and rushing across the courtyard. Zade's hot on his heels.

"Does she know?" Lucca asks.

"Yeah and she's pretty freaked out. She hasn't said anything since I told her."

"Shit! We gotta get her together before the girls find her," Lucca says.

"They know already?" Devya asks, her voice completely panicked.

"Yeah, Bexley's in with the detective now. They're questioning kids one by one in the teacher's lounge," Lucca says.

"Shit! This is going to be bad." Devya bends down and gets in my face. "Fallon, you have to snap out of it. We have to talk about this. The detective is going to want to talk to you and you have to be ready."

That did it. That last line snaps me out of my daze. "Be ready? I'm going to be interrogated by a detective for something that I know I did. I'm not a good liar, Devya. She's going to know."

"Fallon, calm down. She won't know." Devya tries to soothe me again but it doesn't work.

I jump up out of the chair. "She will know. She'll take one look at me and know I'm lying."

Zade, who's been quietly hanging back walks over. He moves in close putting his lips next my ear. "Come with me," he whispers and takes my hand.

I go with him willingly leaving Lucca, Alisander and Devya staring after us with looks of worry clouding their faces.

"Are you taking me to your cabin," I ask.

"Nah. I just wanted to get you away from the three stooges. You were panicking and they weren't helping the situation." He leads me down the pathway leading to Smith hall. He says nothing as we enter the building and make our way to the elevators. We go up to the tenth floor and Zade leads me down the hallway and stops at room 4444. He slips his key in the lock, opens the door and gestures for me to go inside.

Zade's signature scent of black licorice and cola hit me as soon as I step inside. It's all around the space filling the atmosphere with the intoxicating smell. His room is the epitome of bad boy artist cool. His walls are covered in hand painted murals, his furniture and decor is all dark wood and dark colors, there's a canvas with a work in progress on it and his desk is littered with papers of various different sketches.

"Your room is really cool," I say turning to face him.

"Thanks," he says. He's leaning against the door watching me which is always unnerving.

I stare back at him waiting for him to say something but of course he doesn't.

"So, aren't you going to try to convince me to keep quiet," I say.

He sighs and folds his arms across his chest. "Nah. We've already done that dance. I just thought you needed some space."

Zade Amherst - always surprising me. The guy really is a mystery but one thing I do know is that he's good in a crisis. At least where I'm concerned. He seems to always know what I need.

I move around his room looking at the artwork scattered about. I can't get over how good he is. "Your work is so good. You really should be in a gallery," I say looking at him over my shoulder.

He just shrugs.

"I wish I had half the talent you do," I say.

He pushes off the door and comes to stand next to me in front of the half-finished painting sitting on the easel. He picks it up and sits it on the floor and replaces it with a blank canvas. "I think you should paint," he says.

"What?" I say, looking at him sideways. There's a detective on campus questioning students and he wants me to paint.

"Yeah, it'll take your mind off things for a bit." He hands me a palette and paint brush. "You stay here and paint. I actually have to go to class. I've already missed too many days and I don't feel like hearing Professor Jenson's mouth."

"Okay." I have to admit that my nerves have calmed down quite a bit and I'm pretty sure the cool, calm atmosphere in Zade's room has a lot to do with it.

"Stay as long as you like," he says, then leaves.

CHAPTER
TWENTY TWO

I stay tucked away inside Zade's room for hours. The second the paintbrush hit the canvas was a big release for me. Every thought and worry vanished. The only thing that existed was me and the canvas.

I step back to look at what I created so far and I'm in awe. The swirling of dark colors and shadows are new for me. It's like I've taken all my worry, agony and guilt and poured it onto the canvas. It's beautiful. Dark and beautiful.

My cell phone goes off and I sit the palette down and check to see who it is. The number comes up as unknown so I hit the ignore button. The phone starts vibrating again immediately. I stare down at it. It's the same unknown number. This time I answer.

"Fallon, it's Professor Blackmore. Are you okay?"

"Umm…hi. Yes, I'm fine," I say. Why the hell is Professor Blackmore calling me?

"You weren't in your second or third period classes. Your teachers were concerned and reached out to me."

"Why would they reach out to you? Do they know about my sessions with you?" I ask my voice on edge. Isn't therapy supposed to be a private thing?

There's a pause before he speaks. "I like to stay connected with the teachers of the students I'm counseling. It's an important part of the process," he explains.

Apparently, it's a part of the process that he failed to share with me. "Whatever. I'm fine. I just needed some space."

"Did something happen? Is there anything I can do?"

"No, I'm okay. I've been painting," I say.

"Okay, that's good..." there's a long pause before he speaks again. "There's something else. I'm not sure if you're aware but one of our student's Dieter Calais died in a fire. Did you know him?"

My stomach hollows out at the mention of Dieter Calais. I didn't know him. I just killed him. Bile, tart and rancid makes it way up my throat. I close my eyes and swallow, forcing it back down. I have to hold it together. I look at my work in progress sitting on the easel. What a tragic beauty it is but it's also calming. I focus on it.

"Fallon?" Professor Blackmore calls.

"Ummm...no. I didn't know him," I say, somehow sounding normal.

"The authorities seem to think the fire wasn't an accident and they're investing his death. There's a detective here on campus and she needs to speak with you."

My heart takes off like a thoroughbred at a racetrack. The calm and serenity I found in my painting goes completely out of the window and I'm panicking again. Each breath I take feels like the sharp point of a blade pressing against the inside of my chest.

"Why does she want to speak to me?" I ask, choking out the words, trying to sound normal.

"It's just a formality. She's talking to many students," he says.

"Okay. When does she want to meet?" I ask, my heart pounding.

"Now. She's here with me in my office. We thought it best that you meet her here. We figured it would be more comfortable for you." he says.

An overwhelming feeling of dread settles in my stomach. "Okay...I'll head over now," I say and hang up.

The walk to the administration building seems to take forever. It's not really that far from Smith Hall, it's just that I can barely get my feet to move.

"Fallon, wait up!"

I turn to see Devya and Harlyn rushing up the sidewalk behind me.

"Where have you been?" Harlyn says, worry marring her perfectly shaped brow.

"I was at Zade's. Painting," I say as if that's something I normally do.

Both Harlyn and Devya stare curiously at me.

"What's the deal with you and Zade anyway?" Devya asks. Harlyn frowns at her. "Not the time."

"Right," Devya says looking contrite.

"Fallon, where are you going right now?" Harlyn asks.

"Are you going to meet with the detective?" Devya asks.

"Yes," I say, my voice shaky as shit.

"You're not going to tell her anything, right?" Devya asks.

"Just tell her you were at the party with us the whole time. We'll vouch for you," Harlyn says. "You know we got your back. Besides, I've already met with her and told her I was with you and Devya most of the night. Just do the same. Please."

Harlyn and Devya have been my lifelines since coming to Bradford. They embraced me when the rest of the Pure Bloods wouldn't and I appreciate them for that. They're the sisters I never had and I don't want to let them down but I have to do what's right for me.

"You guys have been the two bright spots for me since I came to Bradford. You were both kind to me from the start. You made me feel like I belonged even when I knew I didn't."

"Fallon, you do belong. You're one of us," Devya says, her dark eyes pleading with me to believe her.

"But I'm not though. You all do things in the name of money and family legacy. Me, I'm just a girl from the Midwest who grew up modestly with a mother who loved her. A mother who taught her to always do the right thing. To be the better version of myself as much as I can."

"Fallon, c'mon," Harlyn says, looking at me as if I'm breaking her heart. She braces her hands on either side of my face. "Since you showed up, Bradford has not been the same. You've shaken up the Pure Bloods in the best possible way. And I know that we do things that don't make sense to you. We're all bunch of entitled brats but we love our families and we take care of each other even though we don't particularly like each other. And whether you believe it or not, you are one of us and you can't tell that detective you helped start that fire."

Out of nowhere Bexley rushes over with Indigo trailing behind her. "You better not say a fucking thing to that detective, Stray!" Bexley sneers, pushing Harlyn out of the way and getting up in my face.

"Leave her alone, Bexley," Devya says. "You're not helping things."

"Shut up, Devya. You can't seem to keep your little pet in line so I'll do it," Bexley spits then turns her attention back to me.

She's close to me. Toe to toe in fact and the look she's giving me is murderous. It's enough to make a person shrink away but not me. I've got scarier things to worry about. My freedom hangs in the balance. And not just physically. But mentally too. If I lie to this detective I'll be held captive by that lie for the rest of my life. So, either way I'm a prisoner. I just have to decide which cell I'm willing to reside in.

"Move," I say to Bexley, my voice hard.

Her face tightens and her eyes narrow to angry slits as she stiffens her stance in front of me. "I'm not moving until I know you won't go in there and rat us all out."

"You don't control me. I'm going to do and say whatever I want. Now get out of my way!" I say through clenched teeth before shoving her hard.

I don't think she expected me to do that. She stumbles back and falls to the ground and I move quickly past her towards the entrance to the administration building. I can hear Bexley yelling obscenities at me and the sound of footsteps hitting the pavement behind me.

"Fallon, please don't say anything," Devya yells after me. "You have no idea what will happen if you do. Please. Think of your family. Your grandfather. He's one of us. He took you in. What would he think?"

My steps falter a little. Funny, I hadn't thought about him all this time. I wonder if he knows the task I was given at the Dare Party. If he does, he also knows that I played a part in the death of Dieter Calais. And if that's the case, why hasn't he reached out? Has this all been orchestrated to test me? My loyalty?

I move forward making my way inside the administration building. "I'm going to see Professor Blackmore," I say to the receptionist as I breeze past her towards the elevators.

Lucca slides into the elevator with me just before the doors close causing them to slide back open. Harlyn, Devya, Bexley and Indigo jump inside.

"Hold up," Alisander calls and he makes his way to the elevator.

Zade is right behind him. They both squeeze into the elevator.

I press my back into the wall as they all face me. I feel like a rat in a cage full of vipers. Some friendly. Some not. I look at Devya who stares back at me with eyes full of concern. Then over at Alisander who looks torn between shaking me and comforting me. And Lucca, his brown eyes penetrate me. I can feel everything he feels for me - passion, comfort, uncertainty, anger. Bexley and Indigo, two of the most beautiful girls I've ever seen stare at me, their gorgeous faces contorted in hate.

I look over at Harlyn. Her cool girl demeanor has slipped a bit. She looks worried. Finally, I look at Zade. He's behind the others, back pressed against the elevator wall. His face is neutral, resigned. Yet somehow comforting.

"Did you all come to stop me? To silence me?"

Lucca reaches out grabbing a lock of my hair and fingering it like he does. "We just want to support you."

An unknown sound escapes my throat. I'm not sure if it's a laugh or a cry. "Support me? Really? Because Bexley's over there looking like she wants to murder me."

"You're not wrong about that," Bexley spits.

Lucca shifts his position putting himself in front of Bexley and effectively blocking her from my sight. "You and Bexley are never going to be friends. We all know that but it doesn't matter because you're one of us. The night you completed that dare you became a Pure Blood and we stick together. If you confess to starting the fire you'll take all of us down with you."

"But all of you didn't start the fire," I say.

"True but we all know about it. We all know who started that fire and we've all already talked to the detective." He tilts his head and levels his gaze at me, looking me sure in the eyes. "Fallon, we all lied about that night. So, if you tell that detective the truth, we're all in trouble."

The elevator dings and the elevator doors slide open. The Pure Bloods part opening a path for me to step out. I can feel their eyes on me, weighing me down. Imploring me to do what they want. And I want to. I want to go in there and tell that detective that I was with Harlyn and Devya at the party all night but I've never been the best liar. I'm scared that detective will take one look at me and know what I did. It may just be better to come clean.

"I don't want to hurt you guys. I just…I have to do what I think is right."

"And what is that?" Devya asks.

Before I can answer the door to Professor Blackmore's office opens. "Hello, Fallon," he smiles in that, I'm a therapist, you can trust me sort of way.

"Hi."

He's looks past me at my friends then back at me. "They'll have to stay out here until we're done."

I nod.

"Come on in," he smiles and gestures for me to enter.

My mouth goes completely dry as I move stiffly through the door. I still haven't quite made up my mind about what to do and there's no more time left to think about it. No more time to weigh my options and as I turn to close the door, seven pairs of eyes watch me with suspicion wondering what I'll do.

To be continued...

.

THANK YOU

Thank you so much for reading the first book in the Bradford Academy Series. Honestly, it means the world to me. The Bradford Academy series is a trilogy and book two, titled, HUSH, is in the works and will be available later this year. I can't wait for ya'll to read it.

Bradford Academy Series
Book One: DARE
Book Two: HUSH
Book Three: SPEAK

HIT ME UP

I'd love to connect with you. My main stomping ground is Instagram. Follow me **@authorrowdyrooksy** for updates on the Bradford Academy Series and other novels and projects I'm working on.

You can also hit me up on my website **www.authorrowdyrooksy.com**

Join the Bradford Academy Series commuity on the official Instagram page **@thebradfordseries**

ABOUT THE AUTHOR

Rowdy Rooksy

 Rowdy Rooksy is a writer, film-maker and podcaster who has a love for all things creative. She graduated from college with a degree in International Business but her love for storytelling was too strong to deny so she made the exciting leap into screenwriting and filmmaking. Rowdy has been recognized several times for her screenplays and short films and the natural next step was to venture into writing books and become an author. She loves to read and write romance, erotica, sci-fi, fantasy and YA.

"Don't box me in. I write what I want." ~ Rowdy Rooksy

www.ingramcontent.com/pod-product-compliance
Lightning Source LLC
Chambersburg PA
CBHW032118170626
46808CB00006B/1993